DAR

'Let me try,' said Tracy.

Holly stood back while Tracy pulled as hard as she could. 'It's no good. It won't budge. Sorry, you guys. I guess this door only opens from the outside. I'd say we're stuck!'

Holly's heart turned a somersault. The whole place had been deserted. It could be days, weeks even, before they were found.

She rattled the door handle again. 'It's just got to come open!'

'Shh!' Belinda said suddenly. 'Listen!'

They stood stock still, hardly daring to breathe. From outside came the faint sound of slow, heavy footsteps coming towards the door.

'Oh, lordy, he's come back!' Tracy wailed.

The Mystery Club series

Dark Horse
The Mystery Club 11

Fiona Kelly

Hodder
Children's
Books

a division of Hodder Headline plc

A Catalogue record for this book is
available from the British Library

ISBN 0 340 60727 0

Typeset by Hewer Text Composition Services, Edinburgh
Printed and bound in Great Britain by
Cox & Wyman Ltd, Reading, Berkshire

Hodder Children's Books
a division of Hodder Headline plc
338 Euston Road
London NW1 3BH

1 A mysterious call

'I'm afraid Belinda's gone out. She's riding Melt-down up to the riding centre to get her entry forms for the showjumping competition next week.'

Mrs Hayes was just getting into her sports car as Holly Adams arrived at her friend's luxurious, chalet-style house in the executive part of the pretty Yorkshire town of Willow Dale.

'Thanks, Mrs Hayes. I'll go and find her.' Holly's grey eyes sparkled as she gave her friend's mother a bright smile.

'I'm just off to the hairdresser,' said Mrs Hayes.

Holly thought Belinda's glamorous mother looked as if she'd just emerged *from* the salon. As always, she looked immaculate. Not a single hair was out of place.

A soft breeze ruffled Holly's light brown hair as she stood and watched Mrs Hayes check her make-up in the car mirror, then roar off down the long, gravel drive.

Holly turned her bike round and shot off after her. She'd only called at the house on the off

1

chance. Things seemed to have gone mad at home. Her mum's plan to take a week off from her bank manager's job to decorate the hall hadn't been a great idea. Rolls of wallpaper and ladders were all over the place, and when Holly's younger brother, Jamie, stepped into the bucket of paste Holly reckoned it was time to disappear.

When Mrs Adams had accepted the job at the bank, the family had moved from Highgate into the four-bedroomed cottage in the sleepy town of Willow Dale. Everyone agreed the place needed doing up. But even though Holly's father was a skilled carpenter, he hardly ever seemed to find time to work on the house. Holly's bedroom was still the only organised room in the whole place!

Holly took the road that led up to the Willow Dale Riding Centre. Belinda would be surprised to see her. They hadn't planned to see each other until later, when they'd arranged to meet the third member of the Mystery Club, Tracy Foster, at the ice-cream parlour in town.

Below, Willow Dale was spread out like a map. Holly could see the church spire, the place where the old and new parts of the town met and the distant sprawl of the out-of-town shopping centre and sports complex. It was great living in a place like this; so different from her old home in London where traffic roared day and night and the air wasn't nearly so clean and fresh.

Holly had found it hard to settle here at first but, after hitting on the idea of forming the Mystery Club, things had changed dramatically. Best of all, the only others who had applied to join the club, Belinda Hayes and Tracy Foster, had become her two best friends.

Even then, Belinda had only joined because her mother wanted her to get involved in something that might tempt her away from the television screen. And Tracy had joined because she always belonged to everything!

Since then, the trio had been involved in several real-life mysteries. It wasn't as if they even went looking for them. Mysteries just seemed to find them like bees to a honeypot. It had been the same in Highgate. There, when she was younger, Holly and her two friends, Miranda Hunt and Peter Hamilton, had often found themselves solving real-life mysteries too.

In the distance, Holly could see a horse and rider coming along the road. *That could be Belinda*, Holly thought. She stood on the pedals and waved madly. 'Hi!' she shouted.

Horse and rider trotted briskly towards her.

But to Holly's embarrassment, it wasn't Belinda at all. It was a young woman in her early twenties.

'Morning!' she called. 'Is something wrong?'

Holly gulped. 'Oh, sorry. I thought you were someone else.'

She felt a bit foolish, yelling like that at a perfect stranger. Trouble was, all chestnut thoroughbreds looked alike to Holly.

'Your horse looks just like hers,' she said. 'Sorry.'

'That's OK,' the young woman replied with a smile.

It was really pretty obvious it wasn't Belinda. The rider was much slimmer and had very short black hair beneath her riding hat.

'This is Roddy,' she explained, giving her horse a pat. 'And I'm Jenny Maylam. We live at Snowdrop Farm. It's down in the valley the other side of the hill.'

'He's a great looking horse,' said Holly, although she wasn't really into horses. Mysteries were her great love. She loved reading mystery books and adored watching old black and white mystery movies. Holly hoped to become an investigative journalist one day. She imagined herself writing articles for a top newspaper, perhaps even helping the police solve mysterious crimes. At the moment, though, she had to be content with writing for her school magazine, *Winformation*. The editor, Steffie Smith, had given Holly a regular mystery column and often assigned her to write other articles of interest.

It was Belinda who was the horse-crazy member of the Mystery Club. Sometimes Holly thought

Belinda only lived and breathed for her thorough-bred horse, Meltdown. And Tracy was the energetic one. She was the athletic type, crazy about physical exercise and highly competitive. In fact, if there was any running around to be done Tracy was the first to volunteer.

'Do you live round here?' Jenny Maylam asked Holly.

'I live in the town,' Holly told her. 'I'm on my way to the riding centre to find my friend, Belinda.'

'Well, good luck,' the young woman called cheerily. 'Nice to have met you.' She dug her heels in the horse's flanks and trotted smartly off.

'Bye!' Holly called, pedalling off in the opposite direction.

At the top of the hill, Holly stopped to take a breath. Down in the valley, she could see Snowdrop Farm. A grey horse was just being loaded into a blue cattle truck. The driver put up the tail-gate then got into the cab. From a side road, a green jeep emerged. It waited while the truck pulled out into the road. The truck driver leaned from his cab to say something to the driver of the jeep. Then they parted, both going off in opposite directions.

The truck trundled up the hill towards Holly. She waited on the verge to let it pass. The driver stared at her but ignored her smile. He pulled his tweed cap down over his eyes and roared off down the road.

'That's not very friendly,' Holly muttered to herself, her eyebrows meeting in a frown.

She turned to see the truck branch off where the lane forked. She noticed it was covered in mud as if it had been driving across a field.

At the riding centre, there was no sign of Belinda, although Meltdown was tethered near the horse trough. The green jeep was parked in one of the barns.

The centre's owner, Jake Barratt, a middle-aged man in jodhpurs and a maroon sweat-shirt, was shouting instructions to a group of youngsters having a riding lesson.

Holly went up to a fair-haired girl who was mucking out the stables.

'Hi, have you seen a girl in a faded green sweat-shirt and glasses?' she asked.

'Is she the one who owns that thoroughbred?' The girl indicated Meltdown, his chestnut coat gleaming in the sun. 'She was asking about entry forms for the show.'

'That's the one,' said Holly.

The girl introduced herself as Melanie Brookes. 'We've been admiring her horse,' she said. 'He's fabulous.'

'You'll be Belinda's friend for ever if she hears

you say that,' Holly said. 'Meltdown's the love of her life. Any idea where she is?'

'She's gone into the office with Grant D'Angelo. He's Jake's assistant. He's organising the show.'

'Thanks,' said Holly. 'I'll go and find her.'

She was just about to bound up the steps to the office when there was a cry and a mad clatter of hooves on concrete.

A riderless grey pony suddenly came galloping wildly through the gate. Like lightning, Holly dived forward, grabbing the reins. The pony skidded to a halt, rearing up. The reins were almost torn from Holly's hand. She hung on tight, barely managing to dodge the flying hooves.

At last the pony settled on all fours and stood there trembling.

'Steady, boy!' Holly said breathlessly.

Suddenly a woman rushed through the gate looking distraught.

'Someone come quickly, Kelly's been thrown off!' she cried.

Belinda and a good-looking young man with dark, curly hair and broad shoulders came rushing out of the office. Holly recognised him as the driver of the jeep.

There was a surprised look on Belinda's round face when she saw Holly grimly hanging on to the runaway pony.

'What are you doing here?' Belinda blurted,

7

brushing back a stray lock of straggly brown hair. 'I thought we weren't meeting until this afternoon.'

'Where is she?' the young man was saying urgently to the woman.

'Just down the road,' she gasped.

Holly thrust the reins into Belinda's hands. 'I'll tell you in a minute!'

She bounded up the steps and into the office. Trying to keep cool, she quickly dialled 999. She tapped her foot impatiently as she heard the number ringing at the other end.

'Emergency, which service please?' The operator's voice sounded calm and unruffled.

'Ambulance, please,' Holly said quickly.

The switchboard answered immediately and Holly swiftly told them about the accident and gave the address.

Heart thudding, she ran back out. 'The ambulance is on its way!'

In the road, the young man, whom Holly had realised was Grant D'Angelo, was kneeling beside the small girl lying unconscious on the grass verge. Kelly's mother was crying and wringing her hands.

Holly told Grant what she had done.

Grant threw her a grateful glance. 'Brilliant. Well done!'

Belinda reassured the child's mother. 'The ambulance won't be long, I'm sure.' She pushed her wire-framed spectacles back on her nose.

8

Grant covered Kelly with his jacket. 'We mustn't move her.'

He lifted her hand gently and felt for her pulse. A frown crossed his dark brow. He stood up and put his arm round her mother's shoulders.

'I'm sure she'll be OK, Mrs Harris. Her pulse feels quite steady,' he said reassuringly.

The woman leaned against him. 'Here,' he said kindly. 'Sit down on the verge.'

Belinda sat beside Mrs Harris. 'Try not to worry,' she said. 'I've fallen off loads of times.'

Holly looked at the child's pale face beneath her black riding hat. She glanced at Grant. He shrugged, then took her arm and led her a little way away.

'I don't like it one bit,' he whispered. 'I fibbed to her mum. I didn't want her to panic but the kid's pulse is very weak. I hope the ambulance gets a move on.'

Just then, the sound of a siren came echoing towards them. Holly heaved a sigh. The sooner the little girl was in hospital, the better.

The ambulance screeched to a halt. Two paramedics jumped from the back.

Jake Barratt had run from the yard when he heard the commotion. He stood with the others as Kelly was carefully lifted on to a stretcher and borne away to the local casualty department.

Grant bit his lip. 'I hope she's not badly hurt.'

He turned to Holly and Belinda. 'You feel pretty helpless in a situation like that, don't you?'

'You were brilliant,' said Belinda. 'No one could have done any more than you did.'

'He's always great with kids,' Melanie said. She gave Grant an admiring glance.

Grant shrugged and ran his hand through his dark curls. 'I just like kids, that's all.' He smiled. 'Almost as much as I like horses.' He turned to Holly. 'Are you riding in the show too?'

'No, not me,' said Holly.

Belinda introduced her. 'She'll just come to cheer me on,' she said with a grin. 'What else are friends for?'

By now, Jake had gone back into the office. He poked his head round the door. 'Phone call for you, Grant!'

Grant pressed his lips together and frowned. 'Who is it?' he asked.

Jake shrugged. 'It sounds like the same man who's rung before.'

'Could you tell him I'm not here?'

Jake looked annoyed. 'Grant, this is the third time this has happened. For goodness sake, speak to the man. Maybe then he'll stop pestering you.'

Grant sighed. 'OK.' He disappeared into the office.

'By the way, Belinda,' said Jake. 'Could you tell your mum we collected some jumble for her sale

10

and I left it in your garage yesterday. She may have already found it.'

'No problem,' said Belinda.

Belinda's mother was heavily into raising money for charity. Her latest project was organising a rummage sale in the church hall.

'Well,' said Belinda to Holly when Jake had gone, 'what *are* you doing here?'

'Things are mad at home,' Holly explained. 'I needed a break.'

Belinda pulled Meltdown's reins over his head and mounted. She patted the pocket of her faded green sweat-shirt. She always wore it, usually with a pair of scruffy jeans, despite having a wardrobe full of expensive clothes.

Belinda's parents were rolling in money but as far as Belinda could see, its only advantage was being able to own a thoroughbred horse like Meltdown.

'I've got the entry form,' she said. 'Grant's done me a favour and let me enter the show-jumping, even though the closing date for entries was yesterday.' She groaned. 'It must be way past lunch-time. My stomach's rumbling like a train. I can feel a desire for egg and chips coming on.'

Holly grinned. Belinda was *always* hungry.

She grabbed her bike. 'Come on then, I'll race you home.'

'If I've got the energy,' Belinda sighed.

Just then, Grant came hurtling out of the office with a face like thunder.

'Get all those stables mucked out,' he shouted at a group of girls still discussing the accident. 'It's my day off tomorrow and I want to see it all done before I come back.'

He ran across the yard and jumped into his jeep. The wheels spun as he roared out of the yard and down the drive. Meltdown whinnied in alarm.

'Whoa, boy!' said Belinda, gathering up the reins. She frowned. 'I wonder what's eating him?'

Melanie shrugged. 'He's been having an awful lot of hassle lately,' she said worriedly.

'What about?' asked Belinda.

Melanie shook her head. 'It's a real mystery actually,' she said in a low voice. 'Grant's usually really good-tempered, but since he started getting these phone calls he's been going around like a bear with a sore head.'

At the sound of the word 'mystery', Holly's ears pricked up. She looked at Belinda with a gleam in her eye.

Belinda put her hands on her hips. 'Holly, you've got that look again.'

'What look?' Holly said innocently.

'You know,' said Belinda. 'Your "come on, let's find out what's going on" expression.'

12

'Well,' said Holly, grinning. 'Let's do just that then, shall we?'

Belinda shook her head. 'The things you get me into!'

2 *A missing horse*

'I could almost see your nose twitching when Melanie told us about those telephone calls,' Belinda said to Holly on the way home.

Holly grinned. Belinda was right. She couldn't help wondering just *why* the calls had upset Grant so much.

At Belinda's, Holly sat on the fence while Belinda untacked Meltdown and turned him out. The two friends strolled back across the Hayes's immaculate garden with its colourful shrubbery and rose arbour in one corner.

In the kitchen, Mrs Hayes was briskly preparing lunch. Mr Hayes, a frantically busy, high-powered businessman, was abroad wheeling and dealing as usual.

'Oh, Holly,' Mrs Hayes said as they went in, 'I wanted to see you.' She washed her hands under the tap then smothered them in hand cream. 'Belinda's father has just phoned from Paris. He wants me to go over for a few days and I've managed to book a seat for tomorrow. I wonder

14

if you'd like to come and stay with Belinda while I'm away. Otherwise she'll have to go to her Aunt Susie's for a day or two.'

'Wow, Mum, what a great idea!' Belinda pushed up the sleeves of her baggy sweat-shirt and sat at the breakfast bar. 'You will come, won't you, Holly? And we'll ask Tracy too. We don't want her to feel left out.'

'I'd love to.' Holly said. 'I'd better ask Mum though.'

'Yes, of course.' Mrs Hayes cut herself a thin sliver of Camembert cheese. 'Tell your mother that Susie will always be on call if you need her, and our neighbours will be here all the time. You'll only need to pop across the road to their house if there's an emergency.'

'Right,' said Holly. 'I'll tell her.'

'Go and phone her now.' Mrs Hayes made a shooing motion with her well-manicured hand. 'I want to get everything settled before I start packing.'

Holly went into the thick-carpeted hall to use the phone.

At the other end, Mrs Adams sounded unusually flustered. 'Yes, of course you can, Holly. Tell Mrs Hayes we'll keep an eye on things for her if she'd like us to.'

'Thanks, Mum.' Holly felt full of excitement. It would be great, the Mystery Club spending a few days together.

In the kitchen, Mrs Hayes was telling Belinda that a load of hay had been delivered for Meltdown that morning.

'It was a new man,' she said. 'I just showed him where to stack the bales and left him to it.'

'Mum says it's OK for me to stay,' Holly said as she came back into the kitchen.

Belinda's eyes shone. 'That's brilliant, Holly.' She turned to her mother. 'Mum, could we have a party while you're away?' she said, spreading lashings of butter on a thick slice of bread.

'What kind of a party?' Mrs Hayes looked dubious.

Belinda shrugged. 'Oh, I don't know. Fancy dress or something. We won't make a mess, will we, Holly?'

'No, of course not,' Holly assured Mrs Hayes. 'It would be great if we *could* have a party. We'd clear up afterwards, honestly.'

'Well, all right then. But just a few nice friends, Belinda,' said Mrs Hayes. 'I'll give you the number of my caterers.'

Belinda pulled a wry face. 'I can't see our friends wanting those teensy-weensy little bits of smoked salmon on toast you have at your parties, Mum.'

Belinda's mother gazed at her. 'I suppose you'd rather have those dreadfully fattening fudge-nut sundaes?'

Belinda smacked her lips. 'Yes, please.' Her

eyes lit up. 'Hey, we could have a burger and ice-cream party!'

Mrs Hayes sighed and rolled her eyes to the ceiling. 'I'm sure my caterers will do whatever you wish, Belinda. 'Whether its junk food or *haute cuisine*.'

Belinda chuckled and gave her mother a hug. 'Thanks, Mum. I've got a feeling we're going to have a great time.'

Mrs Hayes drew back, patting her newly-styled hair into place. 'I don't understand you, Belinda. Whenever I throw a party you always moan.'

'That's because you always make me wear one of those awful dresses you buy me.'

Mrs Hayes gave Belinda an expressive look, then sighed.

Holly and Belinda turned up early for their date with Tracy at the ice-cream parlour. They knew she was on her way. When Mrs Hayes had phoned Tracy's mother to ask about Tracy coming to stay, Tracy had already left. Mrs Foster ran a nursery and Tracy had been helping out that morning.

'She's probably exhausted from playing with all those kids,' said Holly, gazing out of the window at the passing traffic.

'Tracy's *never* exhausted,' commented Belinda. 'It makes me tired just thinking about her tearing around everywhere like a cat on hot bricks.'

Holly grinned. 'She's got enough energy for two people.'

Belinda sucked the last of her Coke up through the straw. She sat back. 'True,' she said with a grin. 'I wish she'd get a move on. I'm dying for that sundae!'

Holly looked at her watch then spied Tracy coming down the road. She looked scrubbed and neat as usual in her pink and white track suit.

They got down to the serious business of eating their fudge-nut sundaes before telling Tracy what had happened at the riding centre that morning.

Tracy listened avidly, her eyebrows meeting over her blue eyes in a frown. 'And Melanie said he keeps getting odd phone calls?' she said. 'It sounds kind of mysterious to me.'

'And me,' said Holly. She licked the last traces of chocolate ice-cream from her spoon.

Tracy's short blonde hair bobbed as she shook her head. 'It's a real shame. He sounds a real nice guy, looking after that little kid and all.'

Tracy still had a trace of an American accent even though she'd moved to Willow Dale from California several years earlier. Her English mother had wanted to come back to her own country after she and Tracy's dad divorced.

'He is,' said Belinda. She picked a piece of nut off her sleeve and popped it into her mouth. 'Umm . . . I'm still hungry. I think I'll have

18

another one.' She raised her eyebrows. 'Anyone else?'

'No thanks,' said Holly.

Tracy grinned. 'Belinda, doesn't that stomach of yours *ever* get full?'

'Nope!' Belinda went up to the counter to order another sundae. She came back with a glass brimming with fudge ice-cream topped with chocolate sauce, whipped cream and nuts. She sat down and began tucking in.

'If we could find out who keeps phoning Grant and why,' Holly was saying thoughtfully, 'maybe we could do something to help. After all, it's half-term next week and we'll be pretty bored if we haven't got a mystery to solve.'

'Speak for yourself,' said Belinda. 'I've got to practise for the showjumping. The last thing I want is to get tangled up in one of your webs of intrigue, Holly.'

Holly chuckled. 'Well, Tracy and I can do some investigating while you ride your beloved horse.'

Belinda swallowed a mouthful of ice-cream. 'Not likely,' she said. 'If you two are off on some jaunt I'm coming with you. I'll just have to do some jumping in between.'

'Surely you don't need a lot of practice,' Tracy laughed. 'I thought Meltdown was the best horse in the universe.'

Belinda grinned. 'He is, but it's a good excuse to

get in some extra riding.' She sighed. 'Wow, I am going to be busy . . . the party, the horse show *and* another mystery. I'll need another week off to get over it all!'

At home, Mrs Adams had finished papering one wall.

'Looks great, Mum.' Holly had just come back from town. She stood in the doorway watching her mother. Jamie was trying to get rid of the pieces of wallpaper that were stuck fast to the soles of his trainers.

'I helped,' he said.

'Yes, I bet.' Holly grinned. She'd had experience of Jamie's *helping* before. Where Jamie Adams was concerned, help generally meant getting in the way.

'I did, didn't I, Mum?' Jamie insisted indignantly.

'Yes, Jamie, if you mean getting more glue on yourself than on the wallpaper.' Mrs Adams sighed. 'Go and put the kettle on, please. Your dad hasn't been in from his workshop once this afternoon and I'm sure he'd like a cup of tea.'

'Oh, all right.' Jamie went off muttering to himself.

'Mum?' Holly said later as she and her mother stepped into the kitchen. 'Have you ever heard of someone called Grant D'Angelo?'

Mrs Adams had got to know a lot of people in town through her job at the bank.

Mrs Adams sipped her drink. 'I know an Olivia D'Angelo. She's a customer of mine.'

'It's a pretty unusual name,' said Holly. 'I bet that's Grant's mother.'

'Do you know him then?' Mrs Adams asked.

Holly explained where she had met him. 'It seems as if he might be having some kind of trouble,' she went on. 'We just wondered what, that's all.'

Mrs Adams leaned back in her chair. 'Now, Holly, don't start poking your nose in where it doesn't belong.'

'I'm not going to,' Holly protested.

'I bet you are,' Jamie appeared in the doorway. 'You and Belinda and Tracy are always doing stuff like that. You three can't mind your own business.'

Holly laughed at her brother. 'And *you* can? Get lost, Jamie! Go and watch telly or something.'

Mrs Adams looked at her watch. 'Now, now, you two, I wanted to see the early evening news.' She switched on the kitchen portable.

The local news was on. A reporter was talking to a young woman with short, black hair. Holly recognised her at once.

'Hey, I know that woman! I wonder what's happened?'

21

It was Jenny Maylam, the woman she had met on the way to the riding centre. The interviewer was talking to her outside the gate at Snowdrop Farm.

'My sister's mare was taken in broad daylight,' the woman was saying angrily. 'I just went out for a ride and when I came back she had gone. I just couldn't believe it! I reckon whoever took her was watching the farm and waiting until I went out.'

'Is the horse valuable?' the reporter asked.

The young woman nodded. 'Yes, very. We have several other horses but she was the most valuable. Whoever took her knew exactly what they were doing!'

The reporter turned to the camera.

'So if anyone saw anything suspicious near the Maylams' farm earlier today,' she said, 'please get in touch with the police on Willow Dale 265432.

Holly jumped down from her stool. Her heart began thudding madly. Had she unwittingly witnessed a horse robbery when she was out biking that morning?

'I went by there on my way to the riding centre,' she said excitedly. 'I saw a horse being loaded into a blue truck. Maybe it was the one that got stolen!'

She dashed out into the hall.

'Where are you going?' Mrs Adams called.

'I'm going to tell Belinda and Tracy,' Holly

said excitedly. 'And then I'm going to tell the police!'

'Did you get a good look at the driver?'

The police officer leaned over the counter and stared at the three members of the Mystery Club. They had gone down to the police station to explain about Holly's encounter with the blue truck.

'Yes.' Holly flashed him a brilliant smile. 'He was quite young with a thin face and a ginger moustache and he was wearing a tweed cap right over his eyes.'

The officer frowned. 'If his cap was right over his eyes how come you saw so much of his face?'

'She's very good at details,' said Tracy. 'She's had a lot of practice.'

Belinda leaned against the counter and stared at the policeman.

'Umm . . .' the policeman sat down at his computer. 'OK, start again.'

'I was going up to the Willow Dale Riding Centre,' Holly began. 'And I saw a horse being driven out of Snowdrop Farm in a blue truck. I've told you once.'

The tap-tap of computer keys filled the office. The policeman looked up. 'Did you get the registration number of the truck?'

'No . . . not exactly.' Holly's smile faded a little. The policeman began to look dubious.

'What do you mean, not exactly? Either you did or you didn't.'

Beside Holly, Tracy was fiddling impatiently with the zip on her track suit top.

'I just noticed the number plate was covered in black mud, that's all,' answered Holly.

The policeman leaned his chin on his hand. 'It's not much to go on, you know. Farms always have lorries coming and going and they're generally covered in mud this time of year.' He pressed a key and the screen went blank. He was obviously dismissing them. 'Thanks anyway, girls. I'll check with the Maylams, the horse's owners. It's a pity you weren't more observant.'

'More observant!' Belinda said indignantly, standing up straight. 'She's told you what the driver looked like. Isn't that enough?' She took off her spectacles and wiped them on the sleeve of her sweat-shirt. 'It's a lot more than *some* people would have noticed, I bet.'

The officer looked at Belinda. 'Your friend's description could fit any of a thousand people,' he said. 'Now if someone else had seen the lorry and could confirm what you said . . .'

'Someone did!' Holly said suddenly. 'Grant D'Angelo – he saw it.'

'Grant who?' The policeman began to look more

interested. He called up the computer file once again.

'Grant D'Angelo,' Holly plunged on. 'He works at the Willow Dale Riding Centre. He saw the lorry, *and* spoke to the driver. You ask him.'

'There you are,' said Belinda.

The officer seemed to be having trouble spelling Grant's surname. Eventually he looked up from the keyboard. 'Any idea where this Grant D'Angelo lives?'

Holly shook her head. 'No idea.'

'I know,' Belinda said suddenly. Tracy stopped fiddling with her zip and stared at her.

'Right,' the policeman said, fingers poised over the keys. 'Where?'

'*Casa Blanca*,' said Belinda matter-of-factly.

The policeman tapped in the information.

He looked at Belinda. 'In Spain is it?' he said sarcastically.

Belinda put her hand on her hip. 'No, it's a big white bungalow near the river,' she said. Belinda wasn't easily flustered.

'Right.' The policeman keyed in the information. 'We'll get in touch with Mr D'Angelo. Thanks for telling us.' He grinned at Holly. 'We'll probably find the lorry belongs to the farm, but we'll send someone along to check. Now run along, you girls, I'm sure you've got better things to do than go chasing after horse thieves.'

'Actually, we haven't,' said Holly.

The policeman thought she was joking. 'Well,' he said, 'run along anyway.'

By now a man had come in with a yapping dog.

'What can I do for you, sir?' the policeman said looking past the three girls.

They filed out.

'Great!' blurted Holly. 'Run along, indeed. Anyone would think we were kids.'

'Don't pay any attention to him,' said Tracy. 'He'll soon find out you were right when he talks to Grant.'

They made their way along the high street towards the bus stop.

'And how do you know where Grant lives?' Holly asked Belinda. 'You didn't tell us.'

Belinda shrugged. 'Sorry, I was going to but you rushed down here and I didn't have a chance. My mum told me. She's as good as the telephone directory – *and* she knows everyone's business. I told her I'd met Grant and she said his family moved into the bungalow a while ago.'

When they reached the bus stop, Holly pulled the Mystery Club's red notebook out of her pocket.

'Let's sit down for a minute. I want to write all this down.' She began scribbling a description of the truck and its driver and Grant's name and address.

'Does your mum know anything about Grant's family?' she asked when she had finished.

Belinda shook her head. 'Not really.'

'That's a surprise,' said Tracy with a grin.

'True,' said Belinda drily. 'She did say they keep themselves to themselves – much to her annoyance.'

Just then the bus came along. They clambered aboard and paid their fares.

Tracy was first to get off. 'See you tomorrow,' she said. 'I can't wait to come and stay, Belinda. We're going to have a great time!'

'You bet!' Belinda grinned.

'I'll bring my stuff over in the morning.' Tracy jumped down the steps and ran off towards her terraced house.

Holly was steadying the notebook on her knee and trying to write something else.

Belinda peered over her shoulder. 'What are you writing now?'

Holly frowned and chewed the end of her pen. 'Just a note of that woman's name, the one whose horse was stolen.' She looked thoughtful. 'I'd hate to think it was being pinched right under my nose and I didn't suspect anything. You know what? I think we should ask Grant about that lorry ourselves.'

'Suits me,' said Belinda. 'He said I should come and see his horse sometimes. He told me he's got his own stable at home. It would be a good excuse to call on him.'

'Right, we'll go tomorrow. I'll bring my stuff over to your house in the morning then we'll go, OK?'

Belinda nodded. 'I'll ring Tracy and tell her not to be late.' She rubbed her hands together. 'I just can't wait.'

3 An interesting discovery

Early next morning, Belinda dragged herself out of
bed to see her mother off to the station. Mrs Hayes
was catching the train to London then changing to
the train that went straight through to Paris.

Belinda had made a list of people to invite to
the party. Then she had been trying to phone
them all up. But every time she went to pick
it up it rang with someone wanting to speak to
her mother or father. That was the trouble with
having a mother involved in local society and a
high-powered businessman for a dad. The phone
was always busy.

Eventually Belinda managed to ring everyone on
the list. Only two couldn't come.

Then she carted all the jumble from the garage
to one of the spare rooms.

'We can't have the neighbours seeing it all in
there,' Mrs Hayes had said before she left. 'They'll
think we're starting a junk shop.'

By the time Belinda had finished lugging the
last of a dozen or so bin bags upstairs, she

was exhausted. She had just made herself some banana sandwiches to revive her flagging spirits when Holly and Tracy arrived.

'Are you planning to move in permanently?' she exclaimed as Tracy dumped her camera, three sports bags, a vanity-case and a violin case in the hall.

'I wish!' Tracy said, her blue eyes sparkling. 'It's my sports stuff, three clean track suits, two pairs—'

Belinda rolled her eyes. 'Spare me the details. Come and have a banana sandwich.'

Holly put down her bag and followed them into the kitchen. Belinda was piling the sandwiches on to a plate. 'Come on. We'll take your stuff upstairs and I'll show you your rooms. We'll take these with us.'

'Just think,' Holly said, leading the way. 'A few days without Jamie. I can't believe it!'

'You know you'll miss him,' laughed Belinda.

'Yes,' Holly said. 'Like a hole in the head!'

Belinda thrust open the door to one of the bedrooms. 'Your room, madam,' she said to Tracy.

Tracy gasped. It was the most luxurious guest room she had ever seen. Blue, thick, pile carpet and a primrose satin quilt with curtains to match. 'Wow, is this all mine?' She went and opened the door to the en-suite shower.

'All yours,' Belinda grinned. 'And I know you'll

keep it tidy – which is more than can be said for my room!'

Belinda took Holly to one of the other guest rooms. It was just as big and luxurious as Tracy's. Belinda sat on the antique brass bed tucking into a sandwich while Holly unpacked.

'I've been planning the party,' she said. 'A few friends, loads of food, right?'

'Right.' Holly smiled.

'I've phoned the caterers and all the people on the list. Only a couple said they couldn't come.'

'It's not like you to be so organised,' said Holly. Belinda wasn't one for planning ahead. She tended to take things as they came.

Belinda raised her eyebrows. 'True. I don't know what's got into me,' she said. 'It must be your influence, Holly.'

'You know, if we're going to have a party, we should really be celebrating something,' said Holly.

'How about someone's birthday?' Tracy came bouncing in. She helped herself to a sandwich and sat on the wide window seat that looked out over the garden.

'Good idea,' said Holly. 'Trouble is, it isn't any-one's birthday.'

Belinda looked thoughtful. Then she suddenly grinned. 'Hey, how about Meltdown? He's never had a proper birthday.'

'A birthday party for a horse?' Tracy rolled her eyes. 'OK, Belinda. Anything you say.'

'That's settled then,' said Holly. She always felt better when things were decided. 'Who have you invited?'

Belinda told her.

'If it's going to be fancy dress,' said Holly, 'what on earth are we going to wear?'

'I've just put a load of old clothes and stuff in the boxroom,' said Belinda. 'We could look through that.'

'Great!' Tracy jumped off the bed. 'Let's go!'

It didn't take long to decide. Belinda would go as a scarecrow, Tracy as an Olympic athlete and Holly as the famous fictional detective, Miss Marple.

'This old jacket will do for you, Holly,' said Belinda, holding up a man's tweed jacket. 'Here, try it on.'

Holly slipped it on and twirled round. 'It's a bit big.'

'A *bit* big!' Belinda roared with laughter as Holly looked at herself in the mirror with a comical expression on her face.

'No, if you shorten the sleeves, it'll be perfect,' said Tracy. She held up an old skirt and hat. 'Put these with it and they'll think you really *are* Miss Marple.'

Holly pulled the skirt on over her jeans and stuck the old, battered felt hat on her head.

Ignoring the others' chortles of delight, she stared at herself in the mirror. She stuck her hands into the pockets of the jacket. To her surprise, her fingers closed over a wodge of folded papers. She drew it out.

'Hey, look at this.' She unfolded the papers. 'Betting slips,' she said with a frown. 'And guess whose signature is on them?'

'Superman's?' suggested Belinda, still grinning. 'The jacket looks as if it might have fitted someone his size.'

'Don't be daft, it's Grant D'Angelo. This must be his old jacket.'

There were a dozen betting slips, all with different numbers on. Each one was for ten pounds.

'Wow!' exclaimed Tracy. 'That's a whole lot of money!'

Holly frowned. 'If you win on a horse, do you still keep the betting slips?'

'How should I know?' said Belinda. 'Why?'

'Well, I was just thinking. If Grant put all this money on horses and *lost* he would have been pretty upset.'

'Does it really matter?' asked Belinda. She lay back with a yawn.

Holly shrugged. 'I'm just curious, that's all.' She still looked thoughtful. 'You know, if Grant's lost a lot on the horses, he could owe someone a lot of money.'

33

'What do you mean, *someone*?' asked Tracy looking puzzled.

'Well, a bookmaker.' She waved the tickets. '*This* bookmaker.'

Belinda sat up quickly. 'The phone calls!'

'Exactly,' said Holly.

'Well, if we're going to see Grant, we could ask,' said Tracy.

'He'll probably tell us to mind our own business,' said Belinda.

Holly sighed. 'You're probably right.' She jumped up. 'I still want to ask him about that truck. Hey – how about asking him to the party too?'

'Brilliant!' said Belinda. 'He and I can talk horses all evening.'

'Typical,' said Tracy, smiling. 'We'll do all the work and you'll just have a good time.'

'Nonsense,' said Belinda. 'The caterers are all lined up. All we'll have to do is enjoy ourselves.' She grinned. 'I might even dance if I've got the energy.'

Holly and Tracy laughed.

'That'll be the day,' said Tracy.

'You do know where Grant's house is, don't you?' asked Holly. 'We don't want to spend all day looking for the place.'

'Mum just said it's down by the river, I'm sure we'll find it,' said Belinda.

Before they left, Belinda went to turn Meltdown

out into his paddock. Holly held Belinda's bicycle while she undid the paddock gate and led Meltdown through.

'That's a smart collar,' said Holly. The chestnut thoroughbred was wearing a red head collar with his name in brass studs across the brow band.

'My Aunt Susie had it specially made,' said Belinda. She slapped Meltdown's rump. 'Off you go, baby.' She watched him gallop away, kicking up his heels. His chestnut coat gleamed in the sunshine. Belinda sighed, her eyes full of love. 'Isn't he just wonderful?'

'Wonderful!' the others chorused, rolling their eyes and laughing.

'Come on, Belinda, you can't stay here drooling over your horse,' said Tracy. 'We've got some investigating to do!'

Grant's house was further than they thought. First they had to go right to the other side of town. They took a short cut through the old industrial estate, then rode along past the development of new riverside apartments with their bright window-boxes full of flowers.

As usual, Tracy was in front. Her tanned legs in their white, cycling shorts were going like pistons.

'Does she always have to *race* everywhere?' complained Belinda, too warm in her usual old sweat-shirt and jeans.

'You know she does,' Holly grinned. 'Life's one big competition for Tracy. Hey,' she called, 'wait for us, Tracy. This isn't the *Tour de France!*'

They found the bungalow at last, set in its own grounds, well back from the water's edge.

Tracy stooped by the entrance gate. 'Sorry, you guys.' She beamed as her friends caught her up. In spite of her fast ride she looked neat and cool.

The wrought-iron gates outside *Casa Blanca* were flanked by two white pillars topped by concrete pomegranates. At the end of the drive was a large, sprawling bungalow with white stucco walls and natural wood window frames.

Holly went first to ring on the doorbell.

'It does look like a Spanish villa,' Tracy said, admiring the massive, carved front door. 'I wonder what it's like inside.' She leaned across to try to see through one of the windows.

To their surprise, Grant appeared from round the corner. 'Why don't we go in, so you can find out?' he said, smiling.

Tracy went a bit red. 'Oh!'

'This is our friend Tracy,' Belinda told him with a grin. 'She often puts her foot in it.'

Grant was dressed in a black T-shirt and beige chinos. 'How do you do? Have you come to see Beauty?'

The three girls stared at him. 'Beauty?'

Grant laughed out loud. 'Yes, my showjumper.'

Belinda's eyes lit up. 'Oh, yes! Coming, you two?'

Holly and Tracy hesitated.

'I've got a feeling they'd rather see the house,' Grant said. 'Come on. I'll take you in to meet my mother and she can show you round.'

'Great!' said Tracy.

Grant swung open the front door. The hall was enormous with a polished, wood-block floor and a huge, Spanish fireplace at one end. Ethnic rugs dotted the floor and doors led off in all directions. A huge vase of pink roses stood on the table in the centre.

Holly was so overwhelmed by the size of the place she almost forgot what they had really come for.

'Actually, Grant,' she began, regaining her composure. 'We wanted to ask you . . .'

Just then a woman in a wheelchair came through. She looked surprised to see the three girls standing with Grant.

'I didn't know we had visitors. I was in the conservatory watering my plants.'

Grant introduced them. 'This is my mother, Olivia,' he said. They all shook hands.

'I'm pleased to meet you.' Olivia D'Angelo said graciously. 'I'm always pleased to see Grant's friends.'

37

'Did you know my mother used to be an Olympic champion rider, Belinda?' Grant said proudly.

Belinda's eyes widened. 'Wow! No I didn't. That's great, Mrs D'Angelo!' She had no idea a one-time showjumping champion lived in Willow Dale. Wait until she told her mother *that!*

Grant's mother smiled. She had hair the same colour as Grant's cascading down to her shoulders and dark brown eyes. She held out her long slender hands in a gesture of regret.

'A long time ago, I'm afraid.' She shrugged her thin shoulders. 'But then I had a bad accident and have been like this ever since.'

'A riding accident?' asked Belinda.

Mrs D'Angelo shook her head. 'No. I was flying my light aircraft back from an equestrian conference in France. I hit a storm crossing the channel and the plane crashed.' She looked up at Grant and held out her hand to him. He took it. 'Luckily I had left my son in the care of his nurse. Otherwise he could have been injured too . . . even killed.'

Grant bent to put his arm round his mother's shoulders. 'You can't get rid of me that easily,' he said affectionately. There was no sign of the bad temper he'd shown the day before.

'He's always joking, this boy,' Mrs D'Angelo said. She patted his hand. 'Now take your friends to see Beauty and you can tell them how *you're* going to be an Olympic champion one day.'

Grant flushed, obviously embarrassed. 'Um, yes. OK.'

'Have you been picked for the Olympic team?' Holly asked in a hushed voice.

Grant grinned ruefully. 'No – but my mother lives in hope.'

'It's more than just a hope,' said Mrs D'Angelo. 'It's my dearest wish that Grant should follow in my footsteps.'

Grant shuffled his feet and looked down at the floor.

Tracy sensed his unease and stepped forward. 'Mrs D'Angelo, I'd really love to see this fabulous house if that's OK.'

'Me too,' breathed Holly.

'They're not really into horses,' explained Belinda. 'I'm the only one with any sense.'

Mrs D'Angelo smiled. 'You go to the stable then and I'll take your two friends on a tour of the house. Fran should be back soon. She'll make us some coffee.'

'I wonder who Fran is?' Holly whispered as Mrs D'Angelo wheeled her chair on ahead.

Tracy shrugged. 'No idea. The maid?'

'Don't forget to tell Grant about the party!' Holly called as Belinda went out with Grant.

Mrs D'Angelo took Holly and Tracy through into a room lined with leather-bound books. The sun shone through from the conservatory on to a

39

cabinet full of colourful dolls in all kinds of national costume.

'Grant's father and I collected them from all over the world,' Mrs D'Angelo said when she saw Holly looking. 'He was a diplomat and we travelled a great deal.' Her voice sounded full of regret. 'I missed him terribly when he died, but Grant is a wonderful son and a great comfort to me.'

Holly wandered round, looking at some of the book titles. There were books on equestrian subjects of all kinds – breeding, showing, horse-racing. On the window-sill was a photograph of Mrs D'Angelo on horseback alongside an array of silver cups and shields.

Tracy had gone through into the conservatory. It was full of exotic, scented orchids. 'These remind me of some that grow wild in California,' she said, thinking Holly and Mrs D'Angelo had followed her in.

In the library, Holly heard Tracy's comment and turned to answer her. To her surprise, Tracy wasn't in the library at all. *How odd*, she thought. Tracy's voice seemed to be coming from right behind her.

Mrs D'Angelo smiled at Holly's confusion. Her dark eyes sparkled with mischief. 'Look at this, Holly.' She wheeled herself over to a tiny recess high up in the wall adjoining the conservatory. It was an odd shape, funnelling off to a point. 'This acts as a kind of microphone. When anyone speaks in the conservatory it sounds as if they're right here in this room. We imagine the previous owner had it put in, although we don't know why. It's a good talking point at parties.'

'Yes,' said Holly. 'I bet.'

'Come,' said Mrs D'Angelo. 'I'll take you through into the lounge.'

Through the window, Holly could see Belinda and Grant standing with a huge, black horse. Belinda was fearlessly hugging the animal's neck. In the adjoining paddock there was an assortment of brightly-coloured jumps.

'Grant takes Beauty through her paces every day,' Mrs D'Angelo said when she saw Holly watching them. 'He's already won lots of junior championships. Although he's very modest, he's a brilliant rider. I'm certain he'll get picked for the Olympic team next year.'

Just then, the sound of the front door bell echoed through the hall.

'Excuse me,' said Mrs D'Angelo. She left Holly and Tracy while she went to answer it.

'What a place!' Tracy whispered, wide eyed. 'You could fit my mom's house into the hall.'

Holly grinned. 'Yes, it really is pretty special.'

Mrs D'Angelo returned a moment later. She looked worried and her face had gone pale. 'The police are here,' she said. 'They want to see Grant.

41

Do you think one of you could go and fetch him for me?'

Tracy stepped forward. 'I will, Mrs D'Angelo.' She threw Holly a knowing glance and raced from the room. She dashed down to the stables.

When she told Grant the news he frowned. 'The police! What on earth do they want?'

'I don't know, but you'd better hurry. Your mom looks kind of worried.'

Without another word, Grant hurried back into the house.

'Well, did you ask him?' Tracy said to Belinda.

'Ask him what?' Belinda looked puzzled.

Tracy rolled her eyes. 'About that guy in the blue truck, dummy.'

Belinda pulled her straggly hair out of her eyes. 'We were talking about horses. I would have got round to it eventually.'

'And you didn't mention the betting slips either I guess.'

Belinda chewed her lip. 'No, sorry. I did get round to asking him to the party, though. He said he'd come.'

'Great!' said Tracy. 'Maybe in between talking about horses, Belinda, you could get around to asking about the betting slips *and* those telephone calls.'

Belinda rubbed her nose. 'I'll do my best.'

Indoors, Grant had taken the police officer

through into the conservatory. He barely acknowledged Holly or his mother as he ushered the officer in and closed the door behind them.

Mrs D'Angelo looked at her watch and an impatient frown crossed her face. 'I really don't know where Fran has got to. I'd better make that coffee myself.'

Holly stepped forward, anxious to help. 'I'll do it, Mrs D'Angelo.'

The woman shook her head. 'No, I will. Please sit down and relax. I'm sure Grant won't be a minute. I can't imagine what the police want him for.'

Through the library window, Holly could see Tracy and Belinda heading back towards the house. Suddenly, Holly heard Grant's voice echoing through the niche in the wall.

'No, I'm sorry, I haven't a clue what you're talking about.'

'We just wanted confirmation that you saw a lorry leaving Snowdrop Farm yesterday morning.' The police officer sounded as if he was losing his patience. 'We've got a witness who says she saw you stop and speak to the driver of—'

'Who?' Grant interrupted. 'Who told you that?'

'I'm sorry, sir, I can't disclose that information. We've checked with the farm and they don't know of a lorry answering to the description given to us by the witness. We wondered if you knew the man, or could give us a more detailed description.

You've heard about the theft of a valuable horse, no doubt.'

'Yes, of course I have. Jake Barratt, my employer, told me. But I'm sorry, I didn't see any lorry.'

Holly couldn't believe her ears. What on earth was Grant talking about? She'd *seen* him stop and speak to the driver. She heard the sound of a chair scraping on the tiled floor as someone stood up impatiently.

'I'm sorry,' Grant said sharply. 'I'm very busy right now. I'll see you out.'

To Holly's relief, Grant led the police officer through the conservatory door that led straight into the garden.

She watched them part by the back gate. Grant strode off towards the stables without a backward glance.

Belinda and Tracy came through from the hall. Holly quickly filled them in.

'You're kidding!' exclaimed Tracy. 'You mean he lied to that cop?'

Holly shrugged. 'Yup. I *know* he saw that man in the lorry, yet he denied it completely.'

'That's really odd,' commented Tracy. 'Why on earth would he lie about a thing like that?'

Holly shrugged. 'Search me,' she said.

The three members of the Mystery Club stood in the library, not quite knowing what to do. Mrs D'Angelo had gone to make the coffee and

44

Grant certainly wasn't coming back. They saw him saddle his horse and gallop off across the paddock. It was hardly polite to go hunting round the house looking for his mother but it looked as if they didn't have a choice.

They opened several doors before they found the kitchen.

Mrs D'Angelo was talking to someone on the telephone.

Holly put her head round the door. 'I'm sorry, Mrs D'Angelo,' she said. 'We've got to go now.'

Mrs D'Angelo held her hand over the mouthpiece. 'All right, dear. I'm sorry about the coffee. The phone rang just as I was about to make it.'

'That's OK,' Holly assured her. 'Thanks for showing us round.'

Mrs D'Angelo began speaking into the phone again as Holly shut the door. She caught up with Tracy and Belinda, who were waiting by the front door. They slid out and closed it softly behind them.

'I can't believe it,' Holly spluttered as they made their way through the pillared gateway and back on to the road. She was still puzzled by the blatant lie Grant had told the police. 'What on earth's Grant playing at?'

'He's playing at telling fibs, that's what,' said Belinda matter-of-factly. 'And we've got to find out why!'

4 Trapped!

'*Phew!* Can't we take a breather?' Belinda clambered off her bike and sank down on to one of the seats in front of the riverside block of flats. The Mystery Club was on its way back to Belinda's after their visit to Grant's house.

Holly and Tracy sat down beside her.

'Can you think of any reason why Grant denied seeing that truck?' Holly said. She leaned forward, staring at the water. She had been puzzling over it ever since they left *Casa Blanca*.

'Nope,' said Belinda, polishing her glasses. 'But it's pretty fishy if you ask me.'

'He didn't want the police to know,' said Tracy. 'It doesn't take much brains to work that out.'

'Yes, but why not?' puzzled Holly. 'Surely he'd want a horse thief to be caught. He said he loves horses, remember?'

Belinda shook her head. 'Maybe he *doesn't* want the thief caught.'

'Huh?' Tracy stared at her. 'I don't understand.'

46

'Perhaps he's scared of something?' suggested Holly.

'Scared?' blurted Tracy. 'Scared of what?'

Holly shrugged. 'I don't know, it's just a hunch. But whatever the reason I'd like to find out. The police must have thought I was a complete idiot. That I'd made the whole thing up.'

'If you ask me,' said Belinda slowly, 'our Mr D'Angelo's a bit of a dark horse.'

'The apple of his mother's eye, you mean,' said Holly. 'All that stuff about him being a champion. Is he *that* great a rider, Belinda?'

'She obviously thinks so,' Belinda replied. 'And he certainly looked pretty competent when he galloped away from the house earlier. He's riding Beauty in the show so we'll get a chance to find out then.'

'Meanwhile,' said Holly, 'where do we start trying to figure out exactly what Grant's got to hide?'

'We could ask his friends – they might know,' suggested Tracy.

'Small problem,' said Belinda. 'We don't know who his friends are!'

Holly looked thoughtful. 'I've been thinking,' she said. 'Maybe I could do a piece about Mrs D'Angelo for the school magazine. It could be really interesting. She sounds as if she led a pretty exciting life before her accident. I've been trying to think what I could do for the next edition,' she went on. 'This is a brilliant opportunity to write something about famous people who live in Willow Dale!'

'Like us, you mean,' said Belinda with a grin.

Holly grinned back. 'Well, not *quite* as famous as us.'

'Sounds brilliant,' said Tracy.

'I'm sure I could get her talking about Grant,' Holly said, her eyes bright with enthusiasm.

'That won't be difficult,' said Tracy. 'She really dotes on him. She'll probably tell you his life history.' She jumped to her feet, impatient to be off. Sitting around talking just wasn't her style. 'Come on, you two. Let's go back to the house now.'

'I think I should phone her first, don't you? Maybe ask if I could come over tomorrow?' said Holly.

'I'm making Meltdown's cake tomorrow,' Belinda announced. 'So you can go while I'm doing that.'

The others stared at her.

'Meltdown's *cake*!' Holly chuckled. 'You can't be serious, Belinda.'

Belinda raised her eyebrows. 'Of course I'm serious. You can't have a birthday party without a cake, now, can you?'

Tracy laughed. 'You sure can't! How old is he, Belinda?'

'Eight,' said Belinda. 'So he'll have to have eight candles, right?'

'Right,' said Holly. 'Although I don't see how you're going to get Meltdown to blow them out!'

'And he'd better not be expecting any birthday presents!' said Tracy. She jumped on her bike and strapped on her dayglo orange helmet. 'OK, you guys. Race you home!'

Belinda groaned. 'Oh, no. Here we go again!'

They headed back towards town. Several of the small factories on the old industrial estate had been abandoned when new units were built on the other side of Willow Dale. They were neglected and dirty, some almost falling down. Even in broad daylight the area was silent and deserted.

'This place sure gives me the creeps,' said Tracy, pedalling faster.

'Hey, wait—' Belinda began to protest. Her words were drowned by the sudden appearance of a red estate car hurtling round the bend towards them.

At that point the road was fairly narrow. Tracy skidded to a halt, trying desperately to haul her bike on to the kerb. The others almost cannoned into her.

With a screech of tyres the car swerved to avoid them. Holly caught a glimpse of a surprised face as the driver grappled with the steering-wheel. With a shock, she realised who it was.

The man she had seen driving the truck out of Snowdrop Farm!

Their eyes met and Holly saw the man frown. He had recognised her – there was no doubt about it.

The car straightened up and accelerated away. A shiver passed through Holly as she thought about his pale eyes staring into hers. She had been dimly aware that there was a passenger beside him in the car.

'Quick,' she said to the others. 'Let's go!' She sped off.

'What on earth's wrong?' Belinda shouted.

'That man,' Holly called over her shoulder. 'He's the one I saw in the lorry at Snowdrop Farm. He—' She broke off. There was no time to explain further. The car had spun round and was roaring after them.

'Quick!' Holly swerved off into the carpark of one of the old buildings.

In front, wide doors were open, one hanging half off its hinges. Holly pedalled rapidly inside. The old factory floor was littered with iron girders, broken bits of glass, piles of rubble. But it was too late to avoid them. Holly's front wheel hit a brick with a crunch. She slewed sideways. Her bike went from under her and she landed in a heap amidst the debris.

'Holly!' Behind her, Tracy's voice was almost a scream.

Holly scrambled to her feet. She had scraped her knee but otherwise she was fine.

But the Mystery Club wasn't out of danger yet. The estate car had followed them into the carpark. It skidded to a halt. The door flew open and the man lunged out.

'Hey, you – girl! I want to talk to you!'

Holly didn't wait to hear any more.

'Quick, over here!' she gasped to the others, her heart thudding madly. She had seen a door in the opposite wall – it might lead to safety.

Tracy and Belinda threw down their bikes and tore after her. Holly ran towards a door at the other end, jumping girders and swerving round piles of rubble. All three girls plunged through the door.

Holly turned, her fingers on the handle ready to slam it shut. She saw the dark figure of the man framed in the opposite doorway. He shouted again and waved his fist. His words were lost as Holly put her shoulder to the door and began to push it closed.

'Help me!' she panted.

The others lunged forward, putting their backs against the door. The hinges squeaked and squealed until at last it shut with a dull click.

They were plunged into pitch darkness.

They all leaned against the door, breathing heavily.

Belinda's voice came out of the inky blackness. 'Wow!' She sank to the floor, gasping for breath.

'What do you think he wanted you for?' Even Tracy was out of breath. She felt around in the dark and eventually got hold of Holly's sleeve.

Holly shook her head. 'I don't know. But I wasn't going to wait around to find out.'

Belinda stood up, clutching the air until she came into contact with the other two. They stood together behind the tightly shut door.

'Listen!' Holly whispered. From outside came the faint sound of a car's engine gunning into life.

'He's going.' Holly breathed a sigh of relief.

'He must have seen us come in here,' said Belinda. 'Why didn't he follow and try to get in?'

Holly shrugged in the darkness. 'Perhaps he just wanted to scare us.'

'Scare *you*, you mean,' said Belinda. 'He recognised you, Holly. He knows you saw him come out of Snowdrop Farm. We'd better watch out!'

'Yes,' said Holly grimly. 'That's what I was thinking.'

There wasn't a glimmer of light from anywhere, not even round the edges of the heavy door. The girls were silent for a minute as they waited for their eyes to get used to the darkness.

'What kind of a place *is* this?' whispered Tracy,

straining to see something through the gloom. 'It's black as a coal-mine.'

'I don't know,' Holly said, her heart still pounding. Their voices were echoing eerily round the room as if they were in a vast, empty cavern. She touched one wall. It felt cold and metallic.

'Do you think he's really gone?' Belinda said in a small voice. 'I think I've had enough of hiding in here.'

'Let's wait a little while longer,' said Holly. 'Just in case he's still hanging around outside.'

They huddled together in silence. It was bitterly cold and the dampness seemed to be creeping right into their bones.

'How long have we been in here?' Tracy said at last. 'It feels like hours.'

'If I could see my watch I'd tell you,' said Belinda miserably.

Holly looked at her luminous dial. 'Fifteen minutes,' she said, getting up. 'I'm going to see if the coast's clear. We can't wait in here for ever. We'll suffocate.' She went and pulled at the heavy door handle. It didn't move at all. She pulled again, grunting with the effort.

'Let me try,' said Tracy.

Holly stood back while Tracy pulled as hard as she could. 'It's no good. It won't budge. Sorry, you guys. I guess this door only opens from the outside. I'd say we're stuck!'

Holly's heart turned a somersault. The whole place had been deserted. It could be days, weeks even, before they were found.

She rattled the door handle again. 'It's just got to come open!'

'Shh!' Belinda said suddenly. 'Listen!'

They stood stock still, hardly daring to breathe. From outside came the faint sound of slow, heavy footsteps coming towards the door.

'Oh, lordy, he's come back!' Tracy wailed.

They clutched one another, hearts thudding with fear.

'When he opens the door we'll burst out and make a run for it,' Holly whispered, her mind racing. 'It'll take him by surprise. By the time he's recovered we can be well away.'

The footsteps got closer.

'We'll grab our bikes,' Tracy said, 'and get to the main road as quick as we can.'

Suddenly, there was a rattle from outside and the door hinges began to screech.

Belinda put her hands over her face. She couldn't bear to look.

A crack of light appeared round the edge, as the door opened slowly. Eventually they could see the dark figure of a man standing on the threshold.

Holly took a deep breath. 'OK,' she said, hunching herself up for the rush outside. 'Let's go!'

Together they charged out. There was a shout

of surprise as a man in a dark uniform staggered backwards.

The girls cannoned into him, almost knocking him to the ground. He lost his balance, clutching at the air for support. His dark hat went spinning away across the floor.

'Hey, hey, just a minute!'

Blocking the entrance to the warehouse was a police car. A tall police officer stood beside the open door.

Holly stopped dead in her tracks. She gulped. The police! What on earth were *they* doing here?

'Oops!' Tracy gasped. 'We're really sorry. We thought . . .' She ran to pick up the policeman's hat. She brushed the dirt off and handed it back to him with a sheepish grin.

The first policeman recovered his balance and smoothed back his hair. 'Now, perhaps you'll tell us what you three are doing here?'

Holly, Belinda and Tracy all started talking at once.

The policeman held up his hand. 'OK, OK. One at a time.'

Holly quickly filled them in.

'It was like we told that guy down at the station,' Tracy said, once Holly had explained.

'What guy down at the station?' The policeman looked puzzled.

'The one behind the desk,' Holly explained. 'I

told him I'd seen a blue truck being driven out of Snowdrop Farm the day that horse got stolen.'

'Yes,' said the policeman. 'Go on.'

'And that was him . . . the driver. We met him just along the road and when he saw me he chased us in here,' Holly said. 'He looked really mad.'

'He looked *furious*,' Belinda blurted. 'I thought he was going to kill us!'

'Yes,' Holly said breathlessly, 'Then he locked us in. We were absolutely terrified.'

'And you don't know who he is?' the police officer said with a frown.

'I told you,' Holly said. 'It was the man I saw coming out of Snowdrop Farm.'

'No, no.' The officer tipped his cap to the back of his head and scratched his scalp. 'You don't know his *name*, I mean.'

'No,' said Holly, shuffling her feet.

The policeman shook his head. 'To tell the truth, we haven't been on that case,' he said. 'All we know is that some woman phoned the station a few minutes ago and told us three girls had got locked in the cold-storage room in a derelict warehouse.'

'A woman!' exclaimed Belinda. 'How on earth did a woman know we were in there?'

'He had someone in the car with him,' Holly said. 'It must have been her.'

'You should keep away from these old places,'

56

the policeman warned. 'They're really dangerous. You could have starved to death in there.'

'Starved!' exclaimed Belinda. It was too terrible a fate even to think about.

'We didn't *intend* to come here,' Holly said indignantly. 'We were just innocently cycling past. I told you he chased us.'

The officer wrote a few details in his notebook. 'I'll file a report,' he said. 'And you're absolutely positive you don't know who the man is?'

'No, no idea.' Holly shook her head thoughtfully. She didn't know who the man was but he knew her. He had recognised her as the girl who'd seen him the previous day. He had chased her and left the Mystery Club for dead in an old cold-storage room. No wonder Grant D'Angelo had refused to admit he knew the man. Who would want to be connected with someone as horrible as that?

Holly's scalp went cold. What the Mystery Club had to do now was find out exactly who the man was and why he had so calmly driven away and left them somewhere where they might never be found!

Holly had the feeling that Grant D'Angelo knew the answers to both those questions.

'You realise,' she said to Belinda and Tracy as they resumed their ride home, 'Grant actually *knows* that man, even though he wouldn't admit it to the police.'

'That's just what I was thinking,' said Tracy. 'Not the kind of guy I'd like as a pal, that's for sure.'

'They might not actually be *friends*,' said Holly thoughtfully. 'But they certainly know each other.'

'Well,' said Belinda, pedalling hard to keep up with them. 'It looks like we've got to persuade Grant to tell us who he is then, doesn't it?'

'Right,' agreed Holly. 'So tell me, how exactly are we going to do that?'

5 An interview

The following morning, Holly awoke to a warm shaft of sunlight pouring through the curtains. It made bright patterns on the satin bedspread and across the antique, mahogany dressing-table against the wall. She gazed round at the unfamiliar surroundings, forgetting for a minute that she was staying at Belinda's. Then, suddenly realising where she was, she jumped out of bed.

The smell of toast wafted up the stairway. Holly put on her dressing-gown and slippers and met Belinda, bleary eyed, on the landing. She still looked half asleep.

'Tracy's just left for her morning run,' Belinda mumbled. 'She's made breakfast for us. How anyone can *run* at this time of the morning is beyond me!' She took off her glasses and rubbed her eyes. 'I have enough trouble *walking*.'

'You look like one of the living dead.' Holly grinned.

'Thanks a bunch,' Belinda said good-naturedly. 'Nothing like a compliment to get you going first thing in the morning.' She yawned. 'I'll see you in the kitchen. That toast smells too good to be true.' She stumbled off downstairs, clutching the banister for support.

Holly went to the bathroom and took a quick shower. She dressed in her best jeans and white shirt. If Mrs D'Angelo allowed her to visit she wanted to make a good impression.

On her way to the kitchen, the telephone rang.

'Shall I answer it?' Holly said.

'Go ahead,' Belinda said, her mouth full of toast.

It was Mr Adams. 'I see you're making yourself at home,' he joked when he heard Holly's voice.

'You bet,' said Holly. 'To tell the truth it's great not to have plaster dust in your tea and the sound of Jamie's computer games pinging in your ear!'

Mr Adams laughed. 'Don't get too used to it; you've got to come home sometime.'

Holly chuckled. 'Is that a threat or a promise?'

'A promise,' her dad said. 'Seriously, is everything OK over there?'

'Yes, it's fine.' Holly bit her lip. It really wasn't a good idea to tell her father about the previous day's encounter with the truck driver. He would want her to come home straightaway and that would spoil everything.

'What are you up to today, then?' Mr Adams asked amiably.

Holly told him she hoped to go and interview Mrs D'Angelo.

'That's if she says it's OK,' she added.

Mr Adams sounded impressed. 'I didn't know we had a famous showjumping champion living in Willow Dale.'

'Neither did we,' said Holly. She went on to remind her dad about the party they were having that evening.

'Who are you going as?' Mr Adams asked. Then, before Holly could reply he said, 'No, let me guess . . . Some famous detective . . . Not Miss Marple by any chance?'

Holly laughed loudly. 'Clever you! How did you guess?'

'I wonder,' Mr Adams joked. 'Well, have a good time. Don't forget to ring us if you want anything. If I'm out you can always ring Mum at the bank.'

'I will,' said Holly.

She put the phone down with a sigh. She hated keeping things from her parents but this time it just couldn't be helped.

While she had the phone in her hand, Holly decided to ring Mrs D'Angelo to ask if she could interview her.

'Is it OK if I ring Grant's mum?' she called out to Belinda.

'Sure, go ahead,' Belinda said, still sounding as

if she had her mouth full. 'The phone directory's in the drawer.'

Holly quickly found the D'Angelos' number and dialled.

A woman answered, but it didn't sound like Mrs D'Angelo. Grant's mother spoke quietly, this voice was sharp and businesslike.

'Could I speak to Mrs D'Angelo, please?' Holly asked politely.

'I'm sorry,' said the woman. 'She's a bit tied up at the moment. This is Fran. Can I take a message?'

'Oh,' said Holly. 'This is Holly Adams. My friends and I came to see Grant yesterday and I wondered if I could come and see Mrs D'Angelo again this morning. I write for the school magazine, you see, and I'd like to talk to her about her show-jumping career.'

'Hang on,' said Fran. 'I'll go and ask her.'

Holly heard the telephone being put down, then a door shutting. Minutes later, Fran came back.

'Yes,' she said. 'That'll be fine. It would be better if you come quite soon. There's someone else coming later.'

'Oh, thanks,' Holly said. She almost jumped up and down with joy. This would be a real scoop for the magazine – and the perfect opportunity to find out more about Grant. 'Please tell Mrs D'Angelo I'm really grateful. I'll be there as soon as I can.'

'I shall,' said Fran, putting the telephone down.

Holly found Belinda sitting at the kitchen table poring over a recipe book. Holly rushed in the door, her face flushed with excitement.

'Mrs D'Angelo says it OK to go over this morning.'

'Great!' Belinda said with a mouthful of toast and strawberry jam. She frowned at the book in front of her then wiped off a lump of jam that had slid off her toast on to one of the pages. She licked her finger.

'Fran answered the phone,' Holly went on. 'Mrs D'Angelo mentioned her before, remember?'

'Oh, yes,' said Belinda. She spread another piece of toast with a thick layer of jam. 'We thought she might be the maid.'

'She didn't sound like a maid. More like a secretary or something.'

'Could be,' said Belinda. 'What time are you going?'

'Right after breakfast.'

'You'll find out who Fran is then,' Belinda said absently. She had gone back to poring over her recipe book.

Holly peered over Belinda's shoulder. 'Belinda, what are you doing?'

'I'm looking for a recipe for Meltdown's cake. You know I'm baking it this morning.'

Holly laughed. She had never known Belinda to

bake anything before. 'I thought you were joking,' she commented.

Belinda looked indignant. 'Joking? Of course, I'm not joking.'

'I just hope you're not going to poison everybody,' chuckled Holly.

'Cheek!' Belinda picked up a tea-towel that lay on the table and threw it at her. 'It's going to be absolutely wonderful. You just wait and see!'

The sun was still shining as Holly cycled over to *Casa Blanca*. Parking her bike by the front door, she smoothed down her hair and rang the doorbell. Footsteps came from inside and the door swung open.

A young woman in her mid-twenties stood there. She had the same dark good looks as Grant, except everything about her was drab. She wore a drab beige cardigan and a drab brown skirt. Her black hair was pulled severely back from her face and fixed with an elastic band. Yet it was clear to Holly that with her high cheekbones and dark eyes the woman could look really beautiful if she took more care with her appearance.

The young woman's eyes grew wide, as if she was very surprised to see Holly. Then she quickly seemed to recover her composure.

That's odd, Holly thought. *I did phone first to ask if it was OK to call.*

'Yes?' the woman said sharply. 'Can I help you?' Holly recognised her voice immediately as belonging to the woman who had answered the phone. It seemed more odd than ever that she looked so surprised to see her.

Holly introduced herself. 'I'm Holly Adams. I phoned earlier about coming to see Mrs D'Angelo.'

The woman stood back. 'Oh yes. You'd better come in.'

She went to a door and called through. 'Mother, your visitor's here!'

Holly frowned. *So that's who Fran is,* she thought. How odd. Mrs D'Angelo hadn't mentioned a daughter and Grant hadn't said he'd got a sister. Belinda was right; Grant D'Angelo certainly was a dark horse!

Mrs D'Angelo wheeled herself into the hall, smiling broadly at Holly. She held out her hand.

'How lovely to see you again, Holly. Come through into the conservatory; we can talk there. Oh, by the way, this is my daughter Francesca. We call her Fran for short.'

Holly beamed at Fran. 'I didn't know Grant had a sister!'

'Didn't you?' Fran didn't return Holly's smile.

Mrs D'Angelo wheeled herself towards the conservatory. She turned to look over her shoulder. 'Bring us some coffee, would you, Fran?

Fran held Holly's arm to prevent her from

following. 'Please don't keep my mother talking too long,' she said quietly. 'She tires very easily.'

'I won't,' Holly assured her.

Holly followed Mrs D'Angelo through into the sunny room. She sat down, her notebook on her knee.

'Now, Mrs D'Angelo,' she began. 'Can you tell me about your career in showjumping?'

Ten minutes later, Holly had learned a whole lot about Mrs D'Angelo's past and made lots of notes, but she hadn't got round to mentioning Grant. She had the horrible feeling Fran might reappear any minute to tell her she'd been talking to Mrs D'Angelo long enough. Holly quickly tried to steer the conversation in Grant's direction.

'And you want Grant to follow in your footsteps?' she said.

Mrs D'Angelo nodded. 'Yes, it's my dearest wish.' She looked round impatiently. Fran still hadn't brought the coffee. 'Go and find Fran, will you, my dear? I don't know where's she's got to.'

'Certainly, Mrs D'Angelo.'

Holly left her notebook on the chair. The smell of fresh coffee wafted towards her as she opened the door to the kitchen. The long, narrow room was empty. Holly looked round at the carved oak kitchen units and shelves full of cookery books and tall, thin, glass jars full of different types of pasta. A coffee machine was bubbling away on the worktop but Fran was nowhere to be seen.

Holly went over to the window to see if Fran was out in the garden. There was a notice-board on one wall with various business cards and notes pinned to it. There was a photo of Grant as a small boy on a horse with Fran holding the bridle, looking sulky and fed up. There was a butcher's bill and a list of the doctor's surgery opening hours, a grubby card with *Jack Pierce, Hay and Straw Merchant* written on it and an address and telephone number.

Outside, a car engine started up. Holly craned her neck but couldn't see a vehicle of any kind. Then Fran came in the back door. She flushed when she saw Holly.

'Oh . . . sorry . . . Someone called. I'm just bringing the coffee.'

'I'll take it if you like,' Holly offered.

To her surprise, Fran gazed at her, dark eyes narrowed. 'Exactly what are you doing here?' she asked.

Holly was taken aback. 'I'm sorry, I don't understand, I thought you knew.'

'That you came to interview my mother about her career? Are you sure that's the real reason?'

Holly frowned. What on earth did Grant's sister mean? She couldn't possibly know that Holly had any other motive.

'What other reason could I have?' Holly tried to keep her cool.

Fran shrugged then sat down heavily in a chair. 'I don't know. I just need to protect my mother. She's very fragile you know.'

Holly sat beside her. Her mind raced. Maybe Fran would be the one to pump for information about Grant.

'Yes, I realise that,' she said. 'It's terrible about her accident. Have you always looked after her?'

'Yes,' Fran replied. 'I had to leave school early when my father died. I looked after Grant and my mother.' She rested her chin on her hands. 'I wanted to be an actress, but . . .' Her voice was full of regret. Then she seemed to pull herself together. 'I had to give up that ambition.'

'Surely it's not too late?' said Holly. 'You could still be one if you really wanted to.'

Fran stood up abruptly. 'What I want isn't important!' she said bitterly. 'It's Grant who is going to be the famous one. Didn't my mother tell you she expects him to be picked for the Olympic team?'

'Yes,' Holly said. 'She did mention it. You must be very proud of him.'

Fran shrugged. 'Yes, I suppose I am. We're very close, Grant and I. In fact, I've got him out of trouble more than once.'

Holly's heart thudded. Her luck had changed. This was just what she wanted to hear. 'Oh?' she said casually. 'It's hard to imagine Grant in any kind of trouble.'

'You'd be surprised,' Fran began. Then she stopped and shrugged. 'He's very impulsive. He does things without thinking of the consequences. The problem is, if our mother ever got to find out it would kill her.'

'Find out what?' Holly asked eagerly.

But Fran didn't have the chance to reply. Just then the door opened and Mrs D'Angelo came through. She looked angry. 'Fran, where *is* that coffee? I'm gasping for a cup.'

Fran looked flustered. She rose quickly and bustled about preparing a tray. 'I'm sorry, Mother. Someone came, then I was talking to Holly. I'll bring it through.'

Mrs D'Angelo looked at her watch. 'I'm sorry, Holly. I've got someone else coming in a few minutes. Perhaps we could finish the interview another time.'

Holly nodded her head. 'Of course, Mrs D'Angelo. I'm sorry to have kept you so long.'

Fran went with Holly to the front door. 'You won't say anything to my mother about me getting Grant out of scrapes, will you?' she said. She sounded worried.

'No, of course not,' said Holly. 'But you never did say what kind of trouble he'd been in.'

Fran dropped her gaze. 'No. Well, sometimes my

69

tongue runs away with me. I've probably said too much already.'

'Anything you told me wouldn't go any further,' said Holly. 'I could promise you that.'

Fran seemed relieved. 'No, I know. It's just that any hint of scandal attached to my brother would ruin his chances of getting into the Olympic team. It would kill my mother. That's all she lives for, you see.'

'Yes, I understand,' Holly said calmly. She stood waiting for Fran to continue. Fran was biting her lip and seemed to be trying to decide whether to say anything else or not. Holly got the distinct feeling she would have really liked to discuss her problems with someone. It seemed a lonely kind of life for a young woman, spending her time looking after things for her brother and an invalid mother.

Fran looked as if she was about to continue but then seemed suddenly to change her mind. Instead, she said a brisk goodbye to Holly and showed her to the door.

But Holly wasn't downhearted. Halfway along the drive she let out a great whoop of joy. Although Fran hadn't told her any details, the fact that Grant had been in trouble in the past was enough for now. It might lead to the Mystery Club finding out just *why* Grant had denied seeing that horse thief!

'I've done it,' she shouted to the sky. 'I've really

done it!' Then she sobered up. 'Well – almost,' she added to herself with a grin.

Holly rushed back to Belinda's as fast as she could to tell the others.

Belinda was up to her eyes in cake mixture. Flour was strewn across the kitchen table; there were eggshells on the floor. She was just putting a huge cake tin into the oven. 'I've finished,' she said triumphantly as Holly rushed in. 'You can do the washing-up. I'm going to groom Meltdown before the caterers get here.'

'No . . . wait,' Holly said breathlessly. 'Where's Tracy?'

'Gone out with Kurt to get him a costume for tonight,' Belinda explained. Kurt Welford was Tracy's cricket-mad boyfriend. Besides playing cricket, Kurt was very good at photography. He often took pictures for his father, the editor of the *Willow Dale Express.*

'Never mind, I can tell her later,' said Holly. Now, Belinda, have I got news for you!'

When she had finished telling her what Fran had said about Grant's problems and the need to protect Mrs D'Angelo from any hint of scandal, Belinda frowned.

'That's not much to go on, is it?'

Holly felt deflated. 'Well at least we know he's got a murky past.'

71

Belinda disagreed. 'It's hardly murky. I mean he's not exactly a bank robber or a drug smuggler is he?'

Holly smiled. 'I shouldn't think so.'

'The thing is,' Belinda went on, 'it doesn't look as if Fran's likely to tell us any more. It sounds as if she thought she'd said too much already.'

'True,' Holly agreed.

Belinda put her hands on her hips. 'So who's going to tell us?'

Holly shrugged. 'I don't know,' she said miserably. Holly *hated* mysteries she couldn't solve. 'Although,' she said thoughtfully, 'I really got the feeling she might have poured her heart out to me, given half a chance.'

'Hmm,' said Belinda. She stuck out her bottom lip and frowned. 'Pity you got interrupted then.'

Holly chewed the end of her pencil. 'I wonder . . .' she began.

Belinda wiped a smear of flour off her cheek. 'You wonder what?'

'I wonder if someone else *does* know about Grant. Someone like that truck driver for instance. Someone who might threaten to tell his mother.'

Belinda chewed her lip. 'What, you mean he could be blackmailing Grant?'

'Exactly,' exclaimed Holly. 'That's just what I mean!'

'Hmm.' Belinda bit her fingernail, then grinned

72

broadly. 'You don't think Grant's problems could be anything to do with gambling by any chance, do you? Remember, we found those betting slips in his jacket pocket.'

A broad grin split Holly's face. Her eyes danced with excitement. 'Yes,' she said. 'As a matter of fact, I do.'

'Wow!' Belinda exclaimed. 'Another scoop for the Mystery Club. Wait until we tell Tracy!'

6   A night-time scare

'How do I look?' Holly said later when they were getting ready for the party. She twirled round in her Miss Marple outfit.

'Brilliant!' Belinda was struggling into the old pair of trousers and tattered shirt she'd found for her scarecrow outfit. She pulled a huge turnip wrapped in newspaper out from under the bed. She had drawn a face on it with marker pen and stapled some of Meltdown's straw on top. 'Look, I made a spare head earlier. Good, don't you think?'

'Excellent,' Holly grinned. 'In fact, the hairstyle's better than your own. But why do you need a spare head?'

'Don't you know *anything*?' Belinda said scathingly. 'All the best scarecrows have spare heads. In case their proper one falls off.'

'Oh, pardon me!' said Holly. She pointed to the turnip. 'Actually, I think I like that one best.'

Belinda pulled a face at her. 'Thanks a bunch!'

Tracy came in dressed in her running shorts, spotless white trainers and vest with a number pinned to the front and back. She twirled round and flexed her biceps. 'Looks good, huh?'

Holly and Belinda chuckled. 'The trouble is,' said Holly, 'you look exactly like yourself!'

'So?' said Tracy with a grin. 'I *might* be a famous athlete one day, you never know.'

Belinda rolled her eyes. 'Well at least *I* really look as if I'm in fancy dress!'

'I wouldn't take a bet on it,' Holly chuckled. The old shirt and trousers really weren't that much different from Belinda's usual old sweat-shirt and jeans.

'Talking of bets,' said Belinda, 'I hope Grant turns up. I'm dying to hear more about Beauty.'

'Are we going to mention those betting slips?' asked Tracy.

'I've been thinking about that,' said Holly thoughtfully. 'The best thing would be just to give them back to him and watch his reaction.'

'And how about him and that truck driver?' asked Tracy. 'Should we tackle him about that?'

Holly bit her lip. 'If he's denied it to the police, there's no way he's going to admit it to us.'

'We could just mention it,' suggested Tracy. 'And see how he reacts.'

'This could be a fascinating evening, don't you think, Miss Marple?' said Belinda.

'It might,' Holly said in a mysterious voice. 'We'll have to wait and see.'

The three friends went downstairs to the kitchen. The caterers had laid all the food out on the table. Meltdown's cake was in the centre. Belinda had intended it to be in the shape of a horseshoe but it looked more like a fat, curved sausage. She had iced it bright red.

'It will inspire him to win the showjumping competition,' she said looking at it with pride. 'Winners always get a red rosette.' She turned to the others. 'Looks yummy, don't you think?'

'It looks like a red sausage!' Tracy blurted.

'Thanks a lot!' Belinda put her finger on the top and dug out some icing. She put it into her mouth then smacked her lips. 'Anyway, it tastes great.'

Kurt was the first guest to arrive. He was wearing a fluffy, yellow teddy bear costume with a huge, red, spotted bow tie. The three friends burst into laughter.

'You look great!' Tracy gave him a quick kiss on the cheek.

Kurt pushed back the teddy mask and wiped his forehead. His blond hair stuck out like a brush. 'It's like a sauna inside this costume!' he said with a grin.

Tracy pulled his arm. 'Never mind, you'll survive. Come and help me choose the music.' She dragged Kurt into the drawing-room.

Half an hour later, the lounge was full of friends in all sorts of costumes. In one corner Batman was talking to Cinderella and on the sofa, Dracula was deep in conversation with Snow White.

Grant was the last to arrive. Holly answered the door.

'Hi,' he said. He was dressed in riding gear. 'It's not very original,' Grant said with a shrug. 'But it's all I could think of at short notice.'

'Never mind,' Belinda pushed through from behind Holly. She had her spare scarecrow's head tucked under one arm and a plate of food in the other hand. 'Come through and have something to eat. I want to hear more about that horse of yours.'

Belinda took Grant into the kitchen. Holly followed them.

'I'd like to take a look at Meltdown while I'm here.' Grant helped himself to a sausage on a stick. 'I didn't get a chance to see him properly the other day, what with Kelly falling off her horse. Any chance, Belinda?'

Belinda put down her plate. She had never been known to refuse showing off her horse.

'Sure,' she said. 'We'll go now, and then I'll introduce you to everyone. I've been meaning to ask you about Kelly. Is she OK?'

'She's fine,' said Grant. 'A bit of concussion but nothing worse, thank goodness.'

'I'll come if you like.' Holly grinned at Grant. 'What do you think of my outfit?'

Grant looked amused. 'I've seen that jacket somewhere before, haven't I? I thought I'd given it to the jumble sale.'

'We had a feeling you might recognise it. Here,' Holly held out the betting slips. 'These are yours.'

A wave of colour flooded Grant's face. He snatched the papers from Holly's hand. His eyes narrowed to dark slits as he looked at her.

'Where did you get these?' he asked coldly.

'They were in your pocket – are they important?' Holly said, looking as wide-eyed and innocent as she possibly could.

Grant seemed to get back his composure. 'No, not really.' He grinned sheepishly, then screwed up the slips and threw them into the bin. 'Just a little flutter on the horses, that's all.'

'Little!' blurted Tracy. She and Kurt had been standing at the door, listening. 'There's a hundred pounds' worth there.'

They all turned towards her. Grant flushed again. 'You added them up, then?' he said, raising his dark eyebrows.

Tracy went a bit red. 'Um . . . yeah, I guess we did.'

Grant shrugged. 'Well, just think what I might have won if those horses had come in first. Come on, Belinda. Are we going to see your horse or not?' he said, changing the subject quickly.

'We'll tag along, too,' Tracy said eagerly. She didn't want to miss anything.

It was almost dark as they made their way down to the stable. The sky was covered in thick cloud and a strong wind was blowing.

Belinda switched on the yard lights. She went into the spare table and took a key from its hook behind the door.

'We keep Meltdown locked up at night,' she said to Grant. 'You can't be too careful with such a gorgeous animal.'

'Did you hear about that horse stolen from Snowdrop Farm?' Holly said casually to Grant. 'Terrible, wasn't it? Taken right from under their noses.'

But if Holly thought Grant would give himself away, she was disappointed. He just shook his head and said, 'Yes, what a rotten thing to happen.'

'My dad ran a story in the paper this week,' Kurt piped up. 'Apparently the police haven't got any leads at all.'

'Really?' said Grant. 'That's interesting.'

Meltdown whinnied as they went into the stable. Belinda put her spare turnip head on the manger and went to hug him.

'He's really great,' Grant fondled his ears.

'He's more than great,' said Belinda, looking proudly at her horse. 'He's the best horse in the universe!'

Grant ran his hands over the horse's flanks and down his legs.

'He looks fit as a fiddle,' he said.

'He is,' Belinda said proudly. 'There is not a horse in the country that gets more tender loving care. Is there, pet?'

Meltdown nuzzled her shoulder.

'You should comb your own hair as often as you do his,' Tracy said with a smile. She stroked Meltdown's silky mane.

Grant went back outside to look round the yard. He poked his head into the spare stable where Meltdown's hay was stored.

'It's a nice set-up you've got here, Belinda. Have either of your parents got a horse?'

Belinda snorted and turned to Holly. 'Can you see my mother on a horse?'

'She might mess up her hair!' Holly joked.

Belinda gave Meltdown a last pat. She locked his door and put the key back on the hook.

'Come on. Let's get back before all the food's gone!'

They walked back along the gravel path that ran the full length of the Hayes's huge garden.

Indoors, the party was in full swing. Couples were dancing in the drawing-room. A boy dressed as a Roman emperor was leaning against the door frame drinking a can of Coke. Maid Marion was sitting on the stairs talking to Robin Hood.

'Great party,' Robin doffed his cap at Belinda.

'Is there any food left?' Belinda asked.

'Plenty,' said Maid Marion. 'But no one seems to have been brave enough to try any cake yet, Belinda.'

'Well, we can be the first.' Belinda led Grant off to the kitchen again. 'I made it myself!' she said proudly.

By midnight, everyone had gone. Belinda sank on to the sofa. Tracy had already cleared up and was stacking plates into the dishwasher. Although she'd danced non-stop for hours she was still full of energy.

Belinda yawned. 'Hey, Grant was a pretty cool customer when you showed him those betting slips.'

'He definitely wasn't giving anything away,' Tracy agreed, coming into the room.

'No, but did you see how red he went?' said Holly. 'He recovered pretty quickly but he was certainly embarrassed.'

'Well, he certainly wasn't embarrassed when we talked about that horse getting pinched,' said Belinda. 'Talk about Mr Cool.'

'Maybe he's had a lot of practice,' said Tracy.

'What do you mean?' asked Holly.

'Well, if he has to keep his activities from his mom he must be pretty good at telling fibs. So must Fran. My mom *always* knows when I'm not telling the truth.'

'So does mine,' admitted Belinda. 'Unfortunately.'

'So where does that leave us?' said Holly.

'Not really knowing any more than when we started,' said Belinda. She yawned. 'Let's plan our next move in the morning, shall we? I'm worn out.' She stumbled towards the stairs. 'Night, you two.'

It seemed ages before Holly got off to sleep. The wind whistled round the house and howled through the eaves, and Holly could still hear the party music in her head. Eventually, she managed to drift off to sleep.

But a couple of hours later, she awoke with a start. She'd heard a sound from outside. What was it? A door rattling? The noise of a branch banging against the garage roof? She lay still, hardly breathing. It was all too easy to imagine something creepy in the middle of a stormy night. Her heart was thumping like a drum.

The wind went on screeching round the roof. She figured that must have been what had woken her up.

Or was it?

Holly suddenly had the urge to investigate. She slipped out of bed and tiptoed over to the window.

Outside, the garden was a ballroom of dancing shadows. The wind had blown down a section of fence. Maybe that's what had woken her.

Just then, the moon came out from behind a cloud and Holly's breath caught in her throat. There *was* something out there. Something in the stable yard. She could see a flutter of movement; a shadow, shifting. Her heart flipped. Who on earth was creeping about the stables at this time of night? She decided to go and find out.

She hurriedly shrugged on her dressing-gown and pushed her feet into her slippers. She crept along to both Tracy's and Belinda's rooms. Her two friends were sound asleep. It was a pity to wake them, especially if she'd only imagined seeing things. Besides, Belinda was a notoriously heavy sleeper. Holly doubted if she could wake her without yelling the house down. It was no good – she'd have to go on her own.

Holly grabbed a torch from the kitchen and slipped outside. The rain had stopped. She dashed down the garden. Trees and shrubs seemed to reach out for her. The dancing shadows took on new life. Holly suddenly wished she had stayed safely tucked up in bed. It was crazy, going out in the pitch dark after something that might turn out to be pure imagination.

In the yard, she shone her torch on Meltdown's stable. The door was shut tight. She drew in her breath. The spare stable door was swinging to and fro in the wind. Belinda hadn't shut it properly. That must be what Holly had seen from her window.

She stepped forward to close it. Suddenly the torch went out. She shook it and banged it against her leg, but the switch must have been faulty and the light didn't come on again. Then, to her horror, she heard footsteps behind her. Before she could turn, someone gave her a hard shove in the back.

With a cry, Holly pitched forward, through the open door and into the stable. The torch went spinning away. She fell headlong, landing in a heap against a pile of straw bales.

She clambered to her feet, but it was too late. The stable door had been slammed behind her. She heard someone draw the bolt rapidly across, then footsteps running away.

Holly was trapped!

7   An unlocked door

Holly rushed forward and banged on the stable door.

'Belinda!' she shouted at the top of her voice. 'Tracy! Help!'

Then she fell back. It was no good – they'd never hear her. She'd just have to wait until morning and hope they would come to look for her. But who on earth had been prowling around the yard in the middle of the night?

She had been sitting dejectedly on a bale when suddenly the bolt was drawn back and two pale faces peered in. Torchlight blinded her eyes.

'Holly!' Belinda's voice sounded annoyed. 'What on earth are you up to?'

Holly scrambled to her feet. 'I thought someone was in the yard,' she said breathlessly. 'And when I came out to investigate I got shoved in here!'

Tracy and Belinda glanced at each other then burst out laughing.

'It's not funny, you two,' Holly said indignantly. 'I was scared silly.'

'Oh, Holly, you idiot! It was *me!*' Belinda exclaimed. 'I thought *you* were a prowler.'

'Me!' cried Holly. 'But—'

Belinda took her arm. 'Let's get indoors and I'll explain.'

A few minutes later they sat round the kitchen table, clasping mugs of hot chocolate.

'I woke up with a jump,' Belinda began to explain. 'It must have been you shutting the back door. I looked out of the window and saw someone prowling about with a torch. As I came down the garden, the torch went out and I could see someone standing by the stable. I thought I'd better shove whoever it was inside and wake you two up. But when I got to your room, you weren't there. Then I realised it must have been you I locked in the stable!' Belinda took off her glasses and rubbed them on the sleeve of her dressing-gown. 'Sorry, Holly!'

'I know I was rude about Meltdown's cake but you didn't need to get your own back,' Holly said with a laugh.

'The thing is,' she continued, I really *did* see something out there. But it was only the door swinging in the wind.'

'You've read too many mystery stories; that's your trouble,' said Belinda. 'If you saw the window cleaner with his ladder you'd think he was a burglar.' She yawned. 'All this excitement has tired me out. I'm going back to bed. Coming, you two?'

Holly trailed behind the others as they went upstairs. Although the experience had ended happily, she still felt a sense of unease.

In the morning, Holly again woke with a start. What on earth was it this time? She turned over and looked at the clock. Although it was seven-thirty it seemed only minutes earlier that she'd been creeping down the garden in the pitch dark.

Outside, someone was making a terrible noise and shouting as if they were in real trouble. Holly leaped out of bed and rushed to the window.

Belinda was standing in the garden below. Her hair was a mess, and her face was pale and panic-stricken.

Holly thrust open the window. 'Belinda?' she cried. 'What is it?'

'It's Meltdown,' Belinda shrieked. 'He's gone!'

Holly met Tracy dashing along the landing. 'What's that noise?' she gasped.

'Belinda.' Holly said quickly. 'She says Meltdown's disappeared.'

Outside, Belinda was already rushing back to the stable. Holly and Tracy ran helter-skelter in her wake. They had never seen Belinda run so fast.

In the yard, the door to Meltdown's stable was

wide open. Belinda was walking round in circles, wailing. 'He's gone, he's gone!'

'You're kidding, aren't you?' said Tracy.

'Do I look like I'm joking?' Belinda's face was streaked with tears.

'No,' Tracy said grimly. She went and looked into Meltdown's empty stable.

Belinda had her hands in her hair, and her eyes streamed with tears. 'I came to turn him out and the stable was empty,' she explained between sobs.

'But he was here when we got up last night,' insisted Holly.

'Was he?' Belinda wiped her tears on the sleeve of her sweat-shirt. 'We don't know that for sure. The door was shut but when I looked for the key this morning it was gone. It was in the padlock – look!'

Sure enough, the padlock was still on the door but it was undone and the key was still in it.

'Do you mean he'd gone when we came down here in the night and we didn't know it?' said Tracy. 'That's crazy!'

Holly shook her head. 'I just took it for granted he was in there. I'm sorry, Belinda.'

'I thought that as well. I should have checked.' Belinda burst into tears again. 'What are we going to do?'

'Ring the police!' Tracy was already running towards the house.

Back indoors they sat trying to comfort Belinda until the police arrived.

A police sergeant was there in ten minutes. Hot on her heels came Mr Adams and Jamie. Holly had phoned her father directly they got back indoors.

The police officer introduced herself. 'I'm Sergeant Hadcroft,' she said. 'I've been put in charge of these horse thefts.'

They all went out to the stable. Sergeant Hadcroft took out her notebook.

'Have you touched anything?' she asked Belinda.

'Only the stable door when I opened it this morning.' Belinda sniffed. 'I can't understand why we didn't hear his hooves on the gravel,' she wailed. 'You can't get a horse box down here so they must have walked him right past the house!'

'And you're sure the stable door was locked when you came down in the middle of the night?' the sergeant asked Holly.

Holly shook her head. 'It was closed and I assumed it was locked.'

Jamie had gone off exploring round the back of the stable. He came back with some bits of old sacking and orange baler twine in his hand.

He sat on the fence, practising knots.

'What have you got there, Jamie?' Tracy went to investigate.

Jamie held them behind his back. 'Nothing. Anyway, I found them.'

Tracy frowned. Holly's little brother could really be a pain at times.

'Show Tracy, for goodness sake,' Mr Adams said.

The sergeant was looking around inside the spare stable.

'It's only some old bits of sacking and string.' Jamie tied a piece round his hand and pretended it was a glove puppet. Tracy couldn't help grinning. Jamie could be a real nuisance but he could make you laugh too.

Suddenly, Jamie's face lit up. 'Are these yours, Belinda?'

Belinda frowned. 'Never seen them before.'

'Then I bet the horse thief brought them.'

'What are you talking about, Jamie?' said Holly impatiently.

Jamie waved his fist in the air. 'These bits of sack. I saw it in a film on telly. There was these rustlers and they tied bits of sack round horses' legs to muffle their hooves.' He slipped a piece over his shoe and jumped down to give a demonstration.

Sergeant Hadcroft came out from looking round the spare stable. 'You could be right,' she confirmed. 'It's an old trick. Let's have a look at them.'

Jamie handed her the pieces of sacking. 'See,' he said to Holly, screwing up his nose. '*I'm* better at mysteries than you lot. You didn't even go looking for clues.'

'Give us a chance,' Holly said indignantly. 'We only found out Meltdown had been stolen a quarter of an hour ago.'

The sergeant examined the pieces of coarse material. 'They look just like any old piece of sacking,' she said. 'But I'll take them with me. I'll send them over to the lab at Sheffield. It's possible they'll come up with something. And I'll send someone round to look for fingerprints as soon as possible.'

'Do you think it's the same people that took the other horse?' Holly asked.

The sergeant looked thoughtful. 'I shouldn't be at all surprised. And with two thefts in such a short space of time it looks as if we're dealing with real professionals.'

'Have you found out *anything* about the Maylams' horse?' Belinda asked anxiously.

The sergeant shook her head. 'Not a thing, I'm afraid. By the way, just one more thing. Does anyone else know where you keep the key to Meltdown's stable, other than your friends here and your family?'

Belinda shook her head slowly. 'No, I don't think so.'

'Yes, they do,' Holly said quickly. 'Grant! He was here last night when you unlocked Meltdown's stable. He saw exactly where you hide the key.'

The sergeant looked interested. 'Grant who?'

'Grant D'Angelo,' Holly explained. 'He's a friend of ours. He works at the Willow Dale Riding Centre.'

'Hmm,' said the sergeant, making notes. 'Where does this Mr D'Angelo live?'

Holly gave her the address.

'Well,' said the sergeant, shutting her notebook, 'I'll go and see Mr D'Angelo as soon as I can. Anyone else you can think of?'

'Kurt,' Belinda said suddenly. 'He was here too.' Belinda filled her in.

'It couldn't have been Kurt, now, could it?' Tracy said.

'Hardly,' said Belinda. 'He doesn't know one end of a horse from the other.'

'We have to eliminate everyone from our enquiries,' the sergeant said, writing down Kurt's name and address in her book.

'There are lots of people round here with horses,' said Holly. 'If it really is a gang of professionals they'd all better keep a close eye on their animals.'

'Yes,' agreed the sergeant. 'I'll get some warning notices made. Especially as we've got no real evidence at the moment.' She turned to Belinda. 'You'd better phone your parents and tell them what's happened.'

As soon as they got back indoors Belinda called Mr and Mrs Hayes.

'They're coming back as soon as they can,'

Belinda announced a few minutes later. She sat down heavily on the sofa. 'Mum's upset and Dad's furious.'

Mr Adams got up. 'Come on, Jamie, there's nothing more we can do. Do you want to come home with us, you three?'

Belinda shook her head unhappily. 'No, thanks, Mr Adams. I want to be here in case the police phone.'

Mr Adams patted her shoulder. 'Try not to worry. I'm sure they'll find him.'

'*I'm* not!' groaned Belinda. 'He could be miles away by now. Poor Meltdown. They won't know what to feed him on or anything.' Tears welled up in her eyes once again. Holly went to put her arm round her friend.

'Please try to cheer up, Belinda,' she said comfortingly. 'I'm sure he'll be OK. People pinch horses because they're valuable. They'll know how to look after him.'

Belinda sniffed, then took a tissue to blow her nose. 'I hope you're right.'

When Mr Adams had gone, Holly got out the Mystery Club's red notebook. She jotted a few things down about the theft.

'I didn't say anything to the sergeant,' Holly said, 'but this has just *got* to have something to do with Grant and that man with the lorry. Otherwise, it's too much of a coincidence.'

'That's exactly what I was thinking,' said Tracy.

Belinda turned a tear-stained face towards them.
'I know,' she said miserably. 'But the thing is, what
are *we* going to do about it?'

8   A surprise discovery

A few hours later, Belinda's mother flew in the front door in a whirl of silk scarves and expensive French perfume.

Mrs Hayes threw her arms round Belinda. 'Darling, are you all right? What a dreadful thing to happen. Who do you think did it? What do the police say?'

Belinda emerged from her mother's embrace looking more dishevelled than usual. She straightened her glasses.

'One thing at a time, Mum,' she said. 'Where's Dad?'

Mrs Hayes tutted. 'He couldn't come. He's still got two deals to finalise. He'll be home first thing tomorrow. Belinda, who do you think took poor Meltdown?'

Belinda rolled her eyes. 'If we knew, Mum, then we wouldn't all be standing here like lemons.'

The sound of a car horn came from outside. Mrs Hayes tutted again and opened her leather bag. She took out a twenty-pound note and waved it at Holly. 'Give this to the taxi driver would you, dear? Tell him to keep the change.'

She took Belinda's arm and drew her into the lounge. 'Now tell me *everything*, you girls. From start to finish.'

They told her all they knew.

'Well this Grant *D'Angelo* . . .' Mrs Hayes had a way of expressing her opinion just by her tone of voice. 'He can't have anything to do with it. He lives in that lovely bungalow near the river. He couldn't *possibly* be involved in anything dishonest. Not that I know the family personally but I'm sure they're terribly respectable. The police will have to look elsewhere.' She rose and smoothed down her cashmere sweater. 'In fact, I'm going to phone them and find out just what they are doing to catch these criminals.'

Belinda tried to protest but her mother was already dialling the number. She groaned. Mrs Hayes would have a whole army of police swarming all over the place. It was no good looking *here*. They had to find the man with the blue truck.

The Mystery Club took refuge in Belinda's bedroom. Holly moved aside a pile of horse magazines and dirty socks to sit down.

'Come on, you two,' she said after they'd sat in silence for a minute or two. Belinda was staring out of the window, looking miserable. 'You've *got* to have some ideas.'

'We need to find that lorry,' Belinda said for-lornly. 'But it's like looking for a needle in a haystack!'

Tracy sat cross-legged on the bed. She twisted a lock of hair round her little finger, frowning. 'Needle in a haystack . . .' she repeated slowly.

'What?' said Belinda, turning to face her friends.

'If you wanted to find a farm lorry, where would you look, huh?' Tracy said.

'On a farm?' suggested Holly.

'Hmm,' Tracy was still looking thoughtful. 'Where else?'

'At the cattle market?' suggested Belinda.

'Is there one in Willow Dale?' asked Holly.

'Yes,' said Tracy. 'It's that building with the tower next to the station. There's a market held there a couple of days a week. I went once when Kurt wanted to take pictures of the animals.'

'Which days do they hold it?' said Holly.

Tracy shook her head. 'I can't remember.'

'It'll say in the *Express*.' Belinda hurried down-stairs to get it. Her mother was carrying her suitcases up. She stared in amazement as Belinda ran past.

Belinda came back and spread the paper out on the bed. She turned one or two pages over quickly, then looked up. Her eyes were shining. 'Today!' she said. 'It's today. That's lucky! Come on, you two – what are we waiting for?' She roughly folded the paper and shoved it under her bed.

They rushed down the stairs.

'Wait a minute,' said Belinda at the bottom. 'I've got an idea.'

She disappeared into her father's study and came back with a pair of binoculars.

'We can go up inside the market tower and look through these,' she said. 'You can see the whole place from there.'

'Brilliant!' said Holly.

'Where are you girls off to?' Mrs Hayes called from the top of the stairs.

The girls looked at one another. 'Er . . . we're going to Willow Dale market,' Belinda said.

'The *market*!' Mrs Hayes exclaimed wrinkling her nose. She reached the bottom stair. 'Well, be careful. You get all kinds of people there you know.'

'Yes, I know, Mum.' Belinda assured her. 'We'll be fine, don't worry.'

'Look out for unsavoury types, won't you?'

'Yes, Mum.' Belinda rolled her eyes.

'That's exactly the type we *are* looking out for,' she added when they got outside. She even managed a smile. 'Come on, you two,' she said, full of energy for once. 'Let's get going!'

The cattle market was just outside the main centre

of the town near the railway station. It consisted of a long, narrow building with a tower at one end and rows of pens. Part of the building was filled with noisy calves and other livestock. Crowds of farmers stood talking, discussing the latest prices. A brick building next to the cattle pens housed the auction rooms.

It was almost closing time when the Mystery Club arrived. A stream of lorries loaded with cattle and sheep was coming out. A sign by the gate pointed to the market cafe at the top of the tower.

'Let's go up there first,' Holly said, leading the way. They ran up the stairs and out on to the balcony. Panting, Belinda handed the binoculars to Holly.

'You look. I'm too exhausted!' she gasped.

Holly scanned the market buildings, the cattle pens and the carpark. But there were no blue trucks in sight or any cars that looked like the red estate car they had seen the day before.

Holly shook her head. 'Nothing,' she said disappointedly.

'Let's ask around then,' said Tracy. 'Surely someone's got to know him.'

They went through a pair of glass doors and into the cafe. It was crowded and full of smoke. There was a smell of onions and beefburgers.

'You ask them over there, Belinda.' Holly pointed to a group of farmers sitting at a table in the corner. 'You take that one, Tracy, and I'll ask the waitresses.'

Belinda marched over. The farmers looked at her curiously.

'Sorry to bother you,' she said. 'But I wonder if any of you know a man with a ginger moustache? He drives a blue truck?'

The farmers glanced at one another and shrugged. 'What kind of truck?' one asked, stubbing out his cigarette in the ash-tray.

'Sorry, I don't know,' said Belinda lamely. 'I just know it's blue and the driver's got a ginger moustache.'

The men looked at one another, shaking their heads. 'Sorry, Miss,' another one said. 'I know of several blue cattle lorries but can't think of anyone with a ginger moustache who drives one.'

'He wears a tweed cap,' Belinda said, just remembering. Then she went red. Almost all of the men at the table were wearing tweed caps!

They shook their heads again then went back to their conversation.

Belinda went back to the others, looking down-hearted. 'No luck,' she said miserably. 'How about you two?'

Holly and Tracy shook their heads. 'No,' said Tracy. 'Nobody seems to have a clue who we mean.'

Holly sighed. 'It looks as if we're wasting our time.'

'I'm not giving up!' Belinda said determinedly. 'Not if I have to ask every single person in the whole of Willow Dale!'

They went back down the stairs and out into the market. They were standing by the cattle pens wondering what to do next when suddenly Holly let out a low whistle. She had seen a familiar figure coming through the gate. 'Look!' she whispered. 'See that woman over there? The one in the pink headscarf?'

'What about her?' asked Tracy.

'It's Grant's sister, Fran!' Holly frowned. There was something about that headscarf that set her thinking. She had seen it somewhere before.

'What on earth's she doing at a cattle market?' said Tracy.

'Perhaps she wants to buy a cow?' Belinda said drily.

Fran looked round for a minute or two then headed off in the direction of the lorry park.

'Quick,' said Holly. 'Let's follow her!'

'I can't see what good following Grant's sister round a messy old market is going to do,' Belinda complained, trailing behind.

'Come on!' Holly insisted. 'If my hunch is right you'll soon see.'

'What hunch?' Belinda asked, trotting to keep up with her.

'I've got a feeling Fran's come here to meet someone.'

'Who?' Belinda said.

'Wait a bit and we'll find out,' Holly said mysteriously.

Tracy was already skirting the cattle pens and peering round the corner. Fran had walked briskly across the park and was heading for the timber building on the other side. Suddenly someone stepped out into her path. It was a man dressed in a smart tweed jacket and neat trousers. His ginger hair was combed back smoothly.

Holly recognised him at once. Her hunch had been right. Fran was meeting the man she had seen driving the blue truck away from Snowdrop Farm! The man who had stolen the Maylams' horse!

She nudged the others. 'I thought so!' she exclaimed. 'The man with the blue truck!'

Fran and the man stood talking. Once, he put his arm round her but she shrugged him off. They began arguing heatedly.

'Wow!' whispered Tracy, 'They're having a fight!'

The man started making angry gestures. Fran walked away but he grabbed her and pulled her back.

'I think he's going to hit her!' Tracy cried as the man raised his arm. 'We'd better *do* something!' She made to rush forward.

'No, wait!' Holly held on to her arm. The man was calming down as Fran pleaded with him about something.

'If he's come in his truck he could only have just got here,' Tracy said, staring at Holly. 'How did you know Fran had come to meet him?'

Before Holly could answer. Belinda started forward impetuously. 'I'm going to ask him what he's done with Meltdown!' she cried.

Holly grabbed the back of her sweat-shirt. 'Don't be stupid! Let's see what they do.' Her heart was thumping with excitement.

The man and Fran D'Angelo were still deep in conversation. At last, they parted and he disappeared in the direction of the lorry park. Fran was heading back in their direction.

'Quick!' Holly dodged down behind the cattle pens. 'Don't let her see us!'

They stayed hidden for a minute or two and when they stood up, she had gone.

Tracy's curiosity got the better of her. 'Let's see where *he* went.' She was already running, dodging between the pens, vaulting over straw bales. By the time she reached the corner, a blue truck was just pulling out of the park. It headed off towards the level-crossing.

The others ran up behind her. 'Missed him,' Belinda put her hands on her hips. 'It figures!'

'No, we haven't.' Tracy sped away again. She

ran up the railway-bridge steps, two at a time. She hared across the top, stopping halfway. Underneath, the truck had come to a halt at the crossing gates. As Tracy leaned over the parapet, the lights turned green and the truck roared off down the road.

She jumped up and down and gave the thumbs up sign to the others. She ran back down the steps.

'"Hay and Straw Merchant"!' she said excitedly.

'What?' said Holly and Belinda.

'"Hay and Straw Merchant", dummies. That's what's written on the side of the lorry. Aren't I brilliant?'

Holly gave a whoop of joy. 'Aren't we *all* just brilliant?'

'Fantastic!' said Belinda, still looking miserable. 'One problem, though. There must be dozens of straw merchants round here. So tell me, now what do we do?'

'Tell the police?' suggested Tracy.

Holly shook her head. 'No, not yet. There's still no proof. He'd deny being anywhere near Snowdrop Farm, or your place, Belinda. We've got to find out—' She broke off. A memory had come flashing into her mind.

'What's wrong? asked Tracy,.

'I've just remembered something,' Holly said excitedly. 'I saw a card in the kitchen at *Casa*

Blanca. It said some name then "Hay and Straw Merchant" underneath.'

Belinda and Tracy gazed at her. 'Well?' they chorused.

'Well what?' said Holly.

'What was the name?' said Belinda.

Holly frowned and bit her lip. 'You're not going to believe this, but I've forgotten.'

Belinda sighed. 'That's brilliant, Holly. Some help you are!'

'There was an address as well but I didn't take any notice. Ooh, how stupid!' Holly clapped her hand to her forehead.

'You said it, not me,' said Belinda.

But Tracy had the answer. 'There's only one thing to do then, guys,' she said excitedly. 'We've got to get over to the D'Angelos' and find out what it is!'

As they went through the market gate, someone called out. 'Hey, you girls!'

It was one of the farmers Belinda had talked to in the cafe. He strode over. 'I realised who you must have meant when you'd gone,' he explained. 'I reckon you want Jack Pierce. He's only just grown that moustache and I'd forgotten for the minute. I saw him just now, so I told him three girls were looking for him.'

The Mystery Club looked at one another in horror.

105

'That's absolutely great,' said Belinda after the farmer had walked away again. 'Now he knows we're on his trail. We'd better watch out!'

'What I don't understand,' Tracy said as they rode swiftly over to the D'Angelos' house, 'is how you knew Fran had some connection with Jack Pierce.'

'It was just a hunch,' explained Holly. 'It was that scarf. I suddenly remembered the passenger in that red estate car was wearing one. And the police said a woman had phoned to tell them we were locked in that store. It had to be his passenger; there was no one else about. Then Fran looked *really* shocked to see me when I went to see Mrs D'Angelo . . . Somehow it all just slotted into place.'

'Miss Marple would be proud of you,' Belinda grinned. It was great to see her cheerful again.

'If she's Jack's girlfriend,' Tracy said, 'I bet she was the one who told him about Grant's gambling.'

'His *girlfriend*!' said Holly. 'Well, if she is they certainly don't seem to be getting on very well.'

'To tell the truth,' said Belinda. 'I don't care about any of that. All I want is my horse back!'

When they reached *Casa Blanca* they hesitated in the gateway.

'What are you going to say?' said Belinda as they went up the drive. 'We can't just barge in.'

Holly bit her lip. 'Mrs D'Angelo did say I could

finish the interview sometime. I could say I'd come to do that.'

Tracy shook her head. 'She might think it kind of odd you didn't phone first.'

They got off their bikes and parked them beside the front door. All the windows were closed up and the garage was empty.

'Looks like no one's home anyway,' said Belinda unhappily. 'Now what are we going to do? We've *got* to find out where Jack Pierce lives.' She shook her head. 'We're never going to find Meltdown – I know we're not!' she wailed.

Tracy put her arm round Belinda's shoulders. 'Yes, we are, Belinda. We'll think of something, don't worry.'

'Hey!' said Holly suddenly. She waved the binoculars. 'I vote we creep round to the kitchen window. I bet I'll be able to focus these on that notice-board. It's on the wall opposite.

'Brilliant!' said Belinda, brightening up. 'But we'd better be careful, just in case there *is* anyone in.'

Tracy couldn't wait. 'Let's go!'

The three girls tiptoed round to the side of the bungalow.

Suddenly, there came the sound of a vehicle pulling into the drive.

'Shh!' said Holly. They crouched down in the shrubbery, holding their breath.

A red post van came in through the gate and drove up to the front door. Whistling, the postman got out and pushed a bundle of letters through the letter-box. Then he got back into his van and drove off.

Holly breathed a sigh of relief. She crept out from the bushes and looked round. 'Coast's clear,' she whispered. 'You two stay here and keep a look out. If anyone else comes, whistle.'

'All we need is the window cleaner to turn up now!' whispered Belinda.

Heart thudding, Holly carried on until she came to the kitchen window. It was slightly open. She was just about to stand up when she heard a voice from inside. It was Grant!

Holly slowly rose up until her eyes were just above the sill. Grant was on the phone. Luckily he had his back to her. He sounded angry.

'You've what?' Grant ran his hand through his hair and groaned. 'You're crazy! I *know* that girl. I was at her house last night. What are you trying to do, Pierce? Get me locked up?'

There was silence for a minute then Grant went on. 'No, I've told you, I want nothing to do with it. You can move the horses from your place to wherever you like.' He shook his head. 'Yes, I have got a summons from the bookie's solicitors. How did you know that?' Grant frowned as he listened to Pierce's reply. 'OK, then, don't tell me,' he said angrily. 'Anyway, I'll get the money to pay the debt somehow. I won't resort to horse rustling, that's for sure!'

Grant listened again, a dark frown crossing his brow. Then he shook his head. 'No, I haven't told anyone. But you're really pushing it this time. If you're fool enough to steal another horse in this area then you're crazier than I thought. The police are bound to get on to you. And don't forget, if you tell my mother about the court case then I'll go to the police and tell them about you. Just think about it, will you!'

Grant slammed down the telephone. He stood with his hands on the worktop, taking deep breaths. Then suddenly he turned to face the window.

Holly dropped to the ground. She lay there, hardly breathing. If Grant saw her how on earth was she going to explain why she was spying on him? Her heart was beating like a drum.

The Mystery Club had got it all wrong. It couldn't have been Grant who told Pierce where the key to Meltdown's stable was. He didn't even *know* Meltdown had been stolen until just now! Holly frowned. What on earth was going on?

Suddenly Belinda's voice came in her ear. 'What are you doing, Holly? We thought you'd got caught.'

Holly grabbed Belinda's sweat-shirt and pulled

her down beside her. 'Shh, Grant's in the kitchen. He'll hear you.'

Belinda stood up. 'No, he's not. We've just seen him go up to the stable.'

Holly heaved a sigh of relief. 'Right.' She put the binoculars to her eyes and focused them on the notice-board. 'There it is!' she said excitedly. '*Jack Pierce, Coldblow Farm, High Moor.*'

'Sounds like a fun place,' Tracy joked.

'I wonder where it is?' said Holly.

'My dad's got a really detailed map at home,' said Belinda. 'I bet we could find it on there.'

'Well, wherever it is,' Holly said grimly. 'It's where he's hiding the horses. And if we're going to find them, we'd better be quick. I've just heard Grant say they're going to be moved!'

'Where to?' Belinda gasped.

Holly shrugged. 'He didn't say,' she said. 'And I can tell you something else too, the thefts are nothing to do with Grant after all!'

Tracy and Belinda stared at her in disbelief.

'How do you know that?' said Tracy.

Holly repeated what she had heard.

Belinda looked puzzled. 'So if Grant tells the police he knows Jack Pierce kidnapped Meltdown and the Maylams' grey mare, then Jack will tell Grant's mother about his gambling debts?'

'Right,' said Holly. '*And* Grant's being taken to court. He'll never get into the Olympic team if he's

110

got a criminal record. Pierce knows the news would kill Grant's mother.'

'Wow!' said Tracy. 'But what I can't figure out is how Jack Pierce knew where the key to Meltdown's stables was if Grant didn't tell him?'

Belinda's eyes widened behind the lenses of her glasses. 'The hay merchant!' she said.

'*What* hay merchant?' said Holly.

'The one who brought Meltdown's hay the other day,' Belinda said. 'My mum said it was a new man. She left him to stack the hay in the spare stable. I bet he saw the key hanging behind the door!'

'Brilliant!' said Holly. 'I bet you're right, Belinda. Come on then, you two. Let's get home and find that map!'

9 Frightening encounter

When they got back to Belinda's there was a note from Mrs Hayes. 'Gone to Aunt Susie's,' it read. 'Be back later. Holly and Tracy can stay tonight if they wish.'

'I'd better phone my dad and tell him,' Holly said.

'I'll phone Mom,' added Tracy. 'She'll be wondering where I am.'

According to the large-scale map Belinda found in her father's desk, Coldblow Farm was on top of a hill north of Willow Dale.

'It's miles away,' groaned Belinda. 'It'll take ages to get up there on our bikes.'

'It's not *that* bad,' said Tracy.

'It's all right for you,' Belinda said. 'You never get tired!'

'We could get the bus,' suggested Holly. 'It stops at the end of your road, doesn't it, Belinda?'

'Yes,' said Belinda, looking more cheerful.

Just as they left Belinda's house, a bus came along the road. Belinda jumped off the kerb and waved her arms. The bus stopped and the Mystery Club clambered aboard. They paid their fares and sank down in the back seat.

The bus went through town then bumped and rattled its way up the steep moorland road towards High Moor. On the way, it passed a massive gateway guarded by two large stone lions. At the end of a sweeping drive was an enormous house with towers and turrets stark against the sky.

'Wow!' Tracy peered out of the window. 'That's not Coldblow is it?'

'Don't be daft,' said Belinda. 'It's Chatfield House. Haven't you heard the stories about the Chatfield family? They're notorious around here.'

Holly shook her head. 'I haven't heard about them.'

Belinda shrugged. 'It's ancient history really. The owner had two sons. One was his favourite. He got everything he wanted while the other had to look after the family. The first one was so jealous he killed his brother. The body is supposed to be buried somewhere in the grounds but no one knows where.'

'Wow!' said Holly, her eyes wide.

'It's a bit like one of your mystery stories, Holly,' Tracy said with a smile.

'It is,' said Holly, her eyes gleaming. 'As a matter of fact,' she said, 'the story of that family sounds just like another family I know of – other than the bit about the murder.'

'You mean the D'Angelos?' Tracy asked.

'Yes,' Holly replied. 'Fran made it obvious she was really envious of Grant. She felt he'd had all the lucky breaks while she'd had to give up her ambitions to be an actress to look after their mother.'

'So maybe Fran told Jack Pierce about Grant having to go to court, to get her revenge?' said Belinda.

'Wow!' said Tracy, a broad grin splitting her face in two. 'I reckon we've cracked it!'

'Yes,' Holly said thoughtfully. 'Although she might not have realised Pierce would blackmail Grant with the information.'

'That's true,' the others agreed.

'She told me she sometimes said too much,' Holly reminded them. 'Maybe she'd trusted Pierce and he'd let her down. They *were* having an argument at the market, remember?'

'Anyway,' said Belinda looking downhearted again, 'none of this is helping us find Meltdown, is it?'

They were so busy talking, they didn't realise the bus had stopped.

The driver turned his head. 'Well, are you getting out, you girls, or are you on a round trip?'

'No – we want High Moor,' said Holly.

114

'This is High Moor. We don't go any further.'

'Where's Coldblow Farm then?' said Belinda indignantly.

The driver pointed. 'About three-quarters of a mile further on. Just over that ridge. The road's too narrow for the bus.'

'Three-quarters of a mile!' Belinda exclaimed. 'Do you realise we haven't had any lunch, you two? Someone might have at least suggested bringing a picnic!' She heaved herself out of the seat with a sigh. 'I suppose I'll just have to wait until we get back.'

They watched the bus turn round and head off back towards the town. The sun was low in the sky and the wind had an icy edge. Ahead stretched a narrow, winding road which disappeared over the top of a steep ridge.

Holly hugged herself for warmth. 'Come on, you two, let's get going.'

Standing at the top of the ridge, they could see Coldblow Farm in the valley below. It was a dismal huddle of buildings at the end of a dirt track.

'We'd better go across the field and round the back or someone might see us coming,' suggested Tracy.

They climbed the gate and walked in single file. The ground was wet and squelchy. All three girls felt on edge. Jack Pierce knew someone had been looking for him at the market and it wouldn't take

115

much to guess who it was. If he found them poking around his property, goodness knows what he might do.

Minutes later, all three were crouched behind one of the farm buildings looking across the yard to the house. It looked cold and dreary. The external plaster was cracking and in places, tiles were missing from the roof. Smoke curled from the chimney. A red estate car was parked by the front door. To one side, there was a huge barn with a row of brick-built cattle sheds next to it. Behind that was another ramshackle barn with a door either end.

'I'm going to look in that barn,' said Belinda suddenly. Before the others could stop her, she hurried across the space between two buildings. She swerved to avoid a rusty piece of abandoned farm machinery. One of the barn doors was ajar. Belinda pushed it further open and disappeared inside.

'What's she playing at?' Holly whispered. 'I know she's desperate to find Meltdown, but it's crazy going off on her own. We should stick together, or at least have a plan of action.'

'Too late,' said Tracy. 'She's done it now. Come on. Let's go after her.'

They both leaped to their feet and followed Belinda's footsteps. Holly's heart was hammering. Then she heard Tracy draw in her breath. She came

116

to a dead stop, clutching hold of Holly's arm. Holly froze too.

There came a low, menacing growl from the side of the barn. An evil looking Rottweiler padded round. The dog blocked their way, hackles up, ears flat against its powerful head. It snarled, revealing huge, yellow teeth.

The two girls gulped and clutched at each other.

'Stand still,' Tracy whispered. Beside her, Holly stood rooted to the spot. She certainly wasn't going anywhere!

'Good doggy,' Tracy said in a small voice. 'Nice doggy!'

The animal snarled again.

'He's not listening to you,' whispered Holly.

'Sit!' Tracy commanded in the sternest voice she could muster. 'I read once you should let them know who's boss,' she said.

'He knows very well who's boss,' hissed Holly. '*He* is.'

Opposite, Belinda stood in the barn doorway, her hand over her mouth. Holly prayed she wouldn't do anything silly.

'Should we try to make a run for it?' Tracy said weakly.

'You're joking,' said Holly. Her knees were beginning to feel wobbly.

'Got any other ideas?' said Tracy.

'Let's try walking backwards,' Holly suggested. 'Maybe we won't look so threatening.'

They began to retreat, slowly. The dog snarled again and took a step towards them.

Just then, a woman's voice rang across the yard.

'*Kirk!* Dinner! Where are you?'

The dog's ears pricked up.

'Go on, Kirk,' Holly urged. 'Go and get your nice dinner.' She could see the dog was trying to decide what to do. It stared at them for a second longer then turned and trotted away. Holly let out a huge sigh.

Belinda rushed over once they were out of danger. 'Are you two OK?'

'Great,' said Tracy. 'What happened to *you*?'

'I was just looking round. There's nothing in there but a few old tractors. I went through the back door to the other shed. It's full of cows.'

'Let's take a look in there.' Holly pointed to the other barn. 'It's worth a try. Quick – before Kirk finishes his dinner and decides he wants a pudding!'

Already it was getting dark. The barn looked sinister and brooding in the twilight. Shadows seemed to lurk in every corner. The Mystery Club ran across.

Holly and Tracy heaved open one of the big, sliding doors. The three girls dashed inside and closed it behind them. When their eyes grew accustomed to the gloom they could see one side of the building was full of hay bales.

Belinda clutched Holly's arm. 'Look!'

There parked at the other end was a blue cattle truck!

'That's it, that's it!' Holly's eyes shone. 'That's the one!' They spurted forward. For once, Belinda got there first. The tail-gate was tightly shut and bolted.

Belinda bit her lip. 'It figures!'

From inside came the uneasy shuffling of hooves in straw, then a snort. Belinda stood on tiptoe and peered through the wooden slats. 'It's Meltdown and another horse!' she cried. 'We've got to get them out of there!'

She clambered up on to the rear bumper and began undoing the tail-gate bolts.

But Holly had heard something. Footsteps, coming across the yard. She cocked her head to one side. 'Shh, listen!' she hissed frantically. 'Someone's coming!'

Belinda's hand hovered in mid-air. They all stopped breathing and waited. Seconds ticked by, then one of the huge double doors of the barn began to slide open slowly.

Together they dived for the hay bales, crouching down out of sight.

The door was wide open now. A figure was

silhouetted in the doorway. They knew who it was at once.

Jack Pierce stopped on the threshold. He looked round the barn, his eyes resting on their hiding place. They crouched low, not daring even to breathe.

Then he turned and shouted to someone. 'I won't be long.' He walked the length of the barn then climbed into the cab of the cattle truck and turned on the ignition. The engine gunned into life.

Belinda plucked at Holly's sleeve. 'He's getting away. We've got to stop him!' She started to rise from her crouching position.

Holly pulled her down. 'Don't be stupid, Belinda!'

'But we can't let him get away!'

'There's nothing we can do,' said Tracy. 'It would be crazy to let him see us!'

They watched helplessly as the truck pulled out into the farmyard and headed off down the road.

Beside Holly, Belinda was wailing. 'What did he have to go and do that for?' She got up and stamped her foot. 'He could be taking them miles away! Now what are we going to do?'

'I think,' Holly said grimly, 'we really ought to tell the police this time!'

They ran back along the dirt road to the bus stop. By now, it was almost pitch dark. The three girls huddled together against the wind, stamping their feet to keep warm. Then, to their relief, the bus's headlights swept over the brow of the hill towards them.

'Been up to Coldblow Farm?' It was a different driver this time, a woman with a friendly face.

Holly handed over her fare. 'Yes.'

'She don't get many visitors.' The driver handed Holly her ticket.

'Who don't, er . . . doesn't?' said Tracy, leaping up the steps behind Holly.

'Old Mrs Pierce. Lonely old life she's got. It's as bleak as the Arctic up there in winter. The place is almost falling down, my husband says.'

'I wish it would,' Belinda muttered from behind.

'The old man, Jack's father that was, he drank, you see.' The driver put the bus into gear and moved off. 'Lost all their money. It finished him, losing their other place.'

'Really,' said Belinda. 'What other place?'

'Their other farm. I don't know what it's called. It was before I came here.'

'Oh,' said Belinda.

The bus pulled up at another stop and two more people got on.

'Well, that's definitely his motive then,' Belinda said. 'He's broke. Not that I care. All I want is Meltdown back home.' Once again tears welled up in her eyes.

'We'll get him back,' said Holly. 'I know we will.'

'I wish I was so sure,' sniffed Belinda.

'We will,' said Tracy. 'All we've got to do is find out where Jack Pierce has taken him.'

'And exactly how are we going to do that?' said Belinda, staring miserably out of the window.

'We'll come up with something,' said Holly. 'We always do, don't we?'

'Yes,' Belinda said. 'I suppose so.'

'For a start,' said Holly, 'Wherever it is, it can't be far away.'

Belinda stared at her. 'How do you know that?'

'Didn't you hear what he called out just before he drove off?'

'That's right.' Tracy's eyes lit up. 'He said he wouldn't be long, so he couldn't have been going very far.'

'Exactly,' said Holly.

'But that still doesn't tell us *where*,' wailed Belinda. 'So tell me, you two, what exactly do we do now?'

10 A threat

Mr Hayes's champagne-coloured saloon car purred into the drive first thing next morning. His mobile phone rang twice before he could even unload his bags. His suit was uncreased, his face clean-shaven. He showed no signs of having travelled since the crack of dawn.

When she heard him arrive, Belinda was out the front door in a flash. She waited impatiently while he finished his telephone conversation.

She wrenched open the car door. 'Dad, Dad, guess what's happened now!'

'What?' Mr Hayes got out and opened the boot. He took out two matching, cream, leather suitcases. He slammed the lid down then turned to Belinda. 'Come on, tell me the worst.'

Belinda blurted out a few details of the previous evening's escapade. They went through the front door into the hall. Mr Hayes put his suitcases down with a sigh, then gave Belinda a hug.

'You really shouldn't go off on your own, you know,' he said worriedly. 'It's very dangerous.'

'I wasn't on my own,' said Belinda. 'Holly and Tracy were with me.'

'No,' her father said patiently. 'I mean the three of you. You should leave things like this to the police.'

'We did phone as soon as we got back,' Belinda explained. 'But the sergeant in charge of the case wasn't there.'

Over a fresh cup of coffee the Mystery Club told Mr Hayes the full story of their visit to Coldblow Farm.

'And you say this Sergeant Hadcroft wasn't on duty yesterday evening?' Mr Hayes asked when they had finished.

They shook their heads. Mr Hayes frowned. He wasn't used to people being 'off duty' when he needed them.

'She's there this morning though,' Holly piped up.

'Right!' Mr Hayes stood up. He was accustomed to getting things done, even if it meant working eighteen hours a day to do them.

He went into the hall to use the house phone. Seconds later he came back. 'It's all fixed. They're coming to pick us up. We're going to Coldblow Farm to see just what Mr Pierce has to say for himself!'

Five minutes later Mr Hayes was looking at his watch and pacing the room impatiently. 'What's keeping them? I told them I'd only got an hour to spare.'

But a few minutes later the police arrived. Belinda's father looked with distaste at the panda car that drew up outside the door.

'I'll take my own car,' he said. 'I don't want people to think I've been arrested. You girls go with them to show them the way.'

Sergeant Hadcroft had a colleague with her. A constable. He had sandy-coloured hair and a spotty face.

'I hear you three have been taking the law into your own hands,' he said as they drove up to the farm.

'I was just trying to find my horse,' said Belinda. 'No one else seems to be bothering.'

The sergeant turned round. 'Now that's not true, Belinda. As you know, Mr D'Angelo denied seeing that truck at Snowdrop Farm.'

'He was lying,' Holly said heatedly.

'It was your word against his.'

'So you believed him!' Tracy burst out. 'Why didn't you believe Holly?'

'Because she could have been mistaken. And the fact remains that even if he was lying, we could hardly accuse him of it without any evidence. No one but you saw the truck, or the driver, and the people at Snowdrop Farm haven't a clue who he was.'

'We asked Grant and your friend Kurt about the key to your horse's stable,' said the sergeant. 'Grant said he hadn't noticed where it was and Kurt's mother confirmed he hadn't gone out after arriving home after the party.'

Holly couldn't help grinning. The idea of Kurt Welford being a horse thief was just crazy.

'So I'm afraid we've come to another dead end,' the sergeant said.

'And anyway,' the constable said. 'How do you know it was your horse you saw yesterday?'

Belinda gave him a pitying glance. 'I'd know Meltdown anywhere,' she said.

The constable shrugged. 'Horses all look alike to me,' he said. 'I've got a feeling Mr Pierce isn't going to be very pleased to hear you were trespassing on his property.'

'Would you mind telling me just whose side you're on?' Belinda muttered.

'Give them a break, Pete,' said Sergeant Hadcroft. 'We've been getting nowhere, and if they have found the guilty party, I'll be delighted!'

Fifteen minutes later they pulled up in the farm-yard. Mr Hayes tried to avoid the muddy puddles as he parked beside them. He got out and stared with horror at the state of his saloon car.

'Come on, come on,' he said impatiently as the two police officers got out. 'If you were in business, you'd have lost thousands of pounds by now.'

'You three stay here,' the sergeant said to the Mystery Club. 'We'll call you if we need you.'

In the yard, Kirk was on a long chain. He barked madly as Sergeant Hadcroft led the way to the front door. A grey-haired woman in a black dress covered by an apron answered the door. She stood back to let them in.

In the back of the car, Belinda fiddled with a tear in the knee of her jeans. 'Why wouldn't they let us come along?' she said.

Holly shrugged. 'I haven't got a clue. Maybe they thought we might accuse Jack Pierce of being a horse thief.'

'What's wrong with that?' said Tracy. 'He is!'

Holly shook her head. 'Evidence, Tracy. You've got to have evidence.'

Belinda stared miserably out of the window. The barn door was open and the blue truck was parked where it had been the previous night.

Suddenly Belinda opened the car door and got out. 'Well, I'm not sitting here, waiting,' she said. 'I'm going to look for evidence!'

Before they could argue, she was gone.

Belinda threaded through the puddles and went into the barn.

The truck was parked at one end. Its tail-gate was down, the back empty. Belinda glanced over her shoulder then walked up the ramp. A hay net was tied at one end, under the cab window.

Belinda looked around. Suddenly something caught her eye. There was something in the straw . . . something red. She bent down and pulled it out. It was Meltdown's red head collar!

Belinda gave a cry of triumph. What more evidence did they need? There was Meltdown's name in brass studs across the brow band. There wasn't another head collar like it in the whole of the world!

Belinda was so excited that she hadn't heard someone enter the barn. Heavy footsteps got closer and closer to the truck. Suddenly, a voice rang out.

'I'll take that if you don't mind, Missy!'

Belinda whirled, her eyes wide with shock. Jack Pierce stood on the ramp, one hand outstretched.

Defiantly, Belinda held the head collar behind her back. 'Not likely,' she gulped. 'It belongs to my horse and I want him back. What have you done with him?'

'I don't know what you're talking about,' Jack said evenly.

But Belinda didn't give up so easily. 'Yes, you do!' she insisted loudly.

'Just give that to me, will you!' He stook a step menacingly towards her.

Belinda shook her head slowly. 'No, I won't!'

A flush of anger crept over his face. The veins on his neck stood out.

Belinda felt a lurch of fear. She gulped. Her courage was beginning to wane. Her eyes darted from side to side. There was nowhere to run to. The only escape was past Jack Pierce and no way was he going to let her go until she gave him the head collar. Maybe not even then.

Slowly, the man's hand went to his inside pocket. He drew something out. Belinda gasped. It was a gun. A rather strange looking one with a short, fat barrel.

'Know what this is?' he sneered, waving it in the air.

'A water pistol?' Belinda said sarcastically.

He curled his lip. 'Very funny. It's a gun . . . a special kind of gun.'

'Yeah?' gulped Belinda.

'A stun gun,' he went on. 'The kind you use on animals before you slaughter them. You wouldn't like me to use it on your thoroughbred, would you?'

He came up to Belinda and took hold of her sleeve. He put his face close to hers. She could see his pale eyes glinting. 'N–no,' she stammered.

'So you'd better give me that head collar, hadn't you?'

He put his hand round the back of her and wrenched the head collar from her fingers. 'Right,' he said. 'Now get out and keep your mouth shut or else your horse is dead meat!'

Belinda went cold. An icy fear ran through her. There was no getting away from it – Jack Pierce meant every word he said!

The man gave Belinda a shove. 'Now get going and you haven't seen or heard a thing, right!'

Belinda stumbled down the ramp. She felt peculiar. Her legs were like jelly. She heard Holly calling her.

'I'm just coming,' she shouted hoarsely. She blundered out into the daylight.

Holly saw straightaway that something was wrong. Belinda was looking pale and shaken. She was walking across to the car looking as if she'd just seen a ghost.

Holly took her arm. 'Belinda, are you OK?' She stared at her. 'What's up?'

'I've got to sit down,' Belinda whispered shakily.

She got into the police car and sat hunched up in the back seat. Holly and Tracy exchanged glances and shrugged.

Belinda was just about to tell them what had happened when the two police officers and Mr Hayes came out of the farmhouse.

'Well, that was a waste of time.' Sergeant Hadcroft got back in the car. 'Jack Pierce is in bed with flu. Has been all week, his mother says.'

Holly couldn't believe her ears. 'Didn't you see him then?' she exclaimed indignantly.

'We could hardly drag the poor bloke out of his sickbed, could we? the sergeant said. 'Mrs Pierce promised she'd get him to come down to the station when he's better. I'm sorry, girls, it looks as if this has been a wild-goose chase.'

'But we *saw* Meltdown,' Tracy protested, 'Didn't we, Belinda?'

They all turned to look at her.

Belinda shrugged. 'Oh, I don't know now. It could have been another horse. I'm not sure.'

The others stared at her. Holly started to say something but Belinda kicked her ankle.

'Mrs Pierce said a friend came to collect a horse yesterday,' said the constable. 'They've been looking after it while she's been away.'

'Then she's lying,' said Holly stubbornly.

'We don't know that, Holly,' said the sergeant. 'We can't just accuse an old lady of telling fibs. We said we'd interview Mr Pierce when he's better.'

'I know Mr Pierce's brother,' the constable said as they drove back to Belinda's. 'He was at school with my sister. Of course, they lived over at Hill Beck then. That's before the place caved in.'

The girls looked at one another and shrugged helplessly.

* * *

131

Back at Belinda's Mrs Hayes had returned from her sister Susie's and had gone off to play squash.

Mr Hayes disappeared into his study to make phone calls. 'We'll have to leave it to the police,' he said to the girls before he left. 'And no more wild-goose chases please, you three.'

'OK, Belinda,' Tracy said when Mr Hayes was out of ear-shot. 'What's up? You really look upset about something.'

Belinda told them about her encounter with Jack Pierce in the barn. She repeated his threats. 'And he'll do it, I know he will,' she cried angrily. Tears streamed down her cheeks. 'So I had to keep my mouth shut, didn't I?'

Holly bit her lip. Jack Pierce hadn't been ill in bed at all. His mother was lying to protect him. It looked as if they were dealing with a pretty desperate man.

'Did he say anything else?' Tracy asked, putting her arm round Belinda to comfort her.

'Wasn't that enough?' Belinda replied, sniffing.

'I've been thinking about what that policeman said on the way home,' Holly piped up. 'About the Pierce family living somewhere else years ago.'

'Yeah, that's right,' said Tracy. 'Hill Beck, he called it. He said it caved in or something.'

'Do you think they still own it then?' asked Belinda.

132

Holly shrugged. 'I don't know, but it might be worth finding out.'

'Quick!' said Tracy, eyes shining. 'Where's that map?'

Belinda went into her father's study. He was still on the phone. He frowned as Belinda moved aside a stack of computer print-outs to get at the desk drawer.

'Sorry, Dad,' she whispered. She ran back to the kitchen. 'Got it!' she said.

They spread the map out on the table and pored over it.

'There are so many farms,' wailed Belinda, following the contours of the hills and dales with her finger.

Tracy was frowning. She leaned her chin on her elbows. 'Hey!' she began. 'Oh, no, that's Hill Barn.'

Belinda began to get impatient. She sat back. 'I give up. It's hopeless.'

'No, it isn't,' Holly said triumphantly. She pointed to a dot on the map. 'Look, there it is!'

Belinda peered closer. 'Wow! It's right up on the moor, without even a proper road to it.' She looked at the other two in horror. 'It's *miles*!'

'No, it's not. Look!' Holly said excitedly. She pointed to the map. 'If we cut across the moor it shouldn't take long. But we'll have to hike it. It's too rough for our bikes.'

'Hike!' Belinda protested. Then she gave in with a sigh. 'Well, OK. Anything that will help us get Meltdown back.'

'It might be an idea to take a compass,' Holly said. 'Have you got one, Belinda?'

'There's one in my dad's desk, I'll go and tell him where we're going.' Belinda went back to her father's study. He was still on the phone so she scribbled a note and stuck it in front of him. Then she got the compass and crept out, shutting the door quietly behind her. Mr Hayes hated to be disturbed when he was busy.

'I'll take my camera,' called Tracy already half-way up the stairs to fetch it.

'And this time we'd definitely better take some food,' said Belinda. 'I'll see what I can find.'

Five minutes later they were all set.

In the kitchen, Belinda was filling up a rucksack with hastily made sandwiches. Tracy put in her camera case and the notebook and pen she used to keep a record of all the pictures she took. She put in the compass and quickly buckled up the rucksack.

'OK, you guys,' she said impatiently. 'Let's go!'

11 Lost on the moor

'I'm exhausted,' Belinda said when they were only halfway up the first hill.

'Do you want us to go on our own?' called Tracy. She was way in front as usual, even though she carried the heavy rucksack.

'Not likely. What do you take me for?' Belinda panted.

'Someone who isn't very fit,' Tracy said.

'No one's fit compared to you,' said Belinda. Tracy waited for her to catch up. Belinda undid the rucksack and took out a sandwich. 'This will give me energy,' she said taking a huge bite.

They stopped to look at the map. In front of them, the Vale of York, looking tranquil in the sunlight, stretched into the distance.

'If we branch off left here,' said Holly pointing to a footpath, 'we can take that short cut across the moor, down into the valley then up again.'

'Phew!' said Belinda. 'It'll take hours.'

'No, it won't.' Tracy strode on ahead. 'Come on, slowcoaches!'

135

Holly zipped her waterproof jacket. She frowned up at the sky. The weather was changing. The sun had disappeared and a ghost-grey swirling mist was gathering over the top of the hill, right where they were heading.

Holly shivered. She had heard lots of tales about people being lost on the moors never to be seen again. Then she squared her shoulders. They were only stories. She and Tracy and Belinda would be fine. They'd got the map, a compass *and* food, so there was nothing to worry about.

Minutes later, the first drops of moisture fell on the lenses of Belinda's glasses. She frowned. 'That's all we need,' she said. 'A monsoon!'

'It's only a spot or two,' insisted Tracy. 'A little rain never hurt anyone.' But she sounded less enthusiastic than usual. It *did* look as if the heavens might open at any minute.

The Mystery Club plodded on, keeping close together. They hadn't gone more than another hundred metres when a grey blanket of fine, misty rain enveloped them.

Holly began to feel apprehensive. The rolling landscape that had looked so friendly in sunlight suddenly seemed sinister and threatening. It was easy enough finding the paths in the bright sunlight, but in the grey gloom the tangle of under-growth and paths seemed to merge into one.

'How are we supposed to see where we're

going?' Belinda took off her glasses and wiped them on her sleeve.

Holly studied the compass. 'It's OK, we're heading in the right direction.' She sounded more confident than she felt.

Tracy clutched on to Holly's arm. 'Don't let's get separated. We might never find each other again.'

They walked on in silence. By now, their clothes were soaked and sharp needles of rain stung their faces.

'Sherlock Holmes never had to do this,' moaned Belinda.

'Yes, he did,' said Holly, trying to sound cheerful. 'Remember *The Hound of the Baskervilles*? He and Watson spent hours up on the moors. *They* survived, didn't they?'

'Sherlock Holmes *always* survived,' muttered Belinda.

'Yes, and so does the Mystery Club,' Holly said.

They topped the hill and began the steep descent, following a narrow sheep-path that wound its way round between banks of scratchy heather. The ground was slippery and dangerous. Several times they stumbled, clutching on to one another for support.

The mist was so thick by now that they could only just make out the shadowy figures of one another through the gloom.

Tracy peered into the dimness. 'Oh boy, I hope

this lifts soon. We could end up at Devil's Leap. We'd be over the edge before we knew it.'

'We're nowhere *near* Devil's Leap,' said Holly confidently. 'Just trust me, will you?'

'Just supposing we are heading in the right direction,' Belinda said. 'How far is it now, Holly?'

'I'm not sure,' Holly said, almost wishing they hadn't come. Suddenly, hiking across the moor in a thick mist seemed a pretty silly thing to do.

The ground sloped upwards. Suddenly Tracy grabbed Belinda's arm. 'Shh!'

There was a swish, a rustle, and the pad, pad of feet on turf. An eerie shape was moving towards them. There was a strange sound . . . *baa*.

The three friends burst into laughter. 'Since when have we been scared of sheep?' Tracy said.

A bit further on, the sound of running water reached their ears.

'That must be the beck.' Holly took out the map. 'Yep, this is it. Now we're getting somewhere. You've got to hand it to me; I'm a pretty brilliant navigator!'

'We'll believe that when we actually get there.' said Belinda.

'That's right,' Tracy agreed.

But by the time they reached the edge of the beck, their hearts had sunk. What had looked like a little stream on the map turned out to be a raging torrent. And not metres from where they were standing, the water disappeared into a deep, steep gully. It crashed down the rock fissure with a noise like thunder.

'Great!' said Belinda, her hands on her hips. 'Niagara Falls. Anyone got a barrel?'

'We want to go *across*, not *down*,' said Holly. 'Any bright ideas?'

'Build a canoe?' suggested Tracy.

They stood on the bank, looking across the water with dismay. Holly peered at the map. 'That must be Jacob's Ladder along there,' she said, pointing to the steep gully marked on the map.

'Never mind about that,' said Belinda. 'We need a boat not a ladder.'

'We'll have to wade,' Tracy said determinedly. 'We haven't gotten this far just to give up now.'

'Who said anything about giving up?' Holly began to strip off her shoes and socks.

The others did the same. They stuffed their socks into their pockets, tied their shoelaces together and slung them round their necks.

'I'll go first.' Holly clambered over the rocks, down to the water's edge.

They gasped as the icy deluge hit their legs. Holding hands and leaning against the current they began slowly wading across.

Beneath their bare feet, the river-bed was uneven and slippery. Sharp rocks caught at their toes. Once or twice they turned their ankles as their feet dislodged the stones. They pressed on regardless, leaning forward and clutching on to each other for support.

'Are you two OK?' Holly's voice sounded hollow above the boom of the water.

'Wonderful!' Belinda cried.

Just then a broken branch came hurtling down-stream. It hit a rock, bounced high, then rushed on relentlessly towards them.

Tracy turned just in time to see it bearing down upon them, rolling and tossing as it came. Her eyes widened in horror. The heavy branch was heading straight for them!

'Hey, watch out!' she yelled.

But it was too late. The branch slammed into the back of Belinda's legs. She let go of Tracy's hand as she lost her balance. Her arms windmilled wildly as she struggled to regain her footing.

'Belinda!' Holly threw out her hand and grabbed the back of Belinda's coat. For a minute it looked as if they would both fall into the raging water. Then, gradually, they both regained their balance.

'Phew!' Belinda shouted. 'Not really the weather for a swim!'

Holly grinned. Together they pressed on, hands clasped. Eventually, they reached the far bank. They clambered out and fell to their knees, pant-ing.

'Wow!' gasped Tracy. 'Are you two OK?'

'Wonderful,' said Belinda, wringing water from the hem of her jacket.

'Great!' said Holly, looking with dismay at her soaked jeans. 'I'll probably get pneumonia but aside from that I'm fine.'

'Right!' Belinda got to her feet with uncharacteristic energy. 'How far now, Holly? Meltdown's up here somewhere and we've got to find him!'

Holly pulled out the map. 'To be honest, I'm not sure.'

'Don't say we're lost,' said Belinda.

'It would help if we could see where we were going,' protested Holly. She struggled to her feet. 'I *think* we're heading in the right direction.'

They marched in silence. The ground was soft and seemed to wobble beneath their feet. Long spiky grass grew in tufts beside the muddy path and a bitter, acrid smell rose from the turf. Their feet made squelching noises and their shoes seemed to be sinking further down with each step they took.

'*Hey!*' Holly gave a cry. Her feet had sunk right down. Black, oozing mud covered her shoes to the ankles. She tried to lift her foot up but it was stuck fast. There was a gurgle and the earth seemed to seethe and boil like a volcano. Suddenly both feet sank further. Holly began to struggle but with each movement she went down a bit more.

Then there was a bubbling sound like water

141

going down a plug hole and she was sucked in right up to her knees.

Holly threw out her arms in panic. 'Help – I'm going right down!'

Belinda and Tracy stared at their friend in horror.

'Oh, no,' Belinda wailed. 'Tracy! What are we going to do?'

'Quick!' Tracy threw herself flat on the ground, pulling Belinda down with her. She stretched out her arms. 'Grab my hands, Holly. Hold on!'

They both grabbed Holly's hands, pulling with all their might. But it was impossible to pull her out. The bog was sucking Holly further and further down.

'It's no good,' she panted. 'I'm not moving.'

'Pull!' Tracy gasped.

At last, Holly felt the mud begin to give up its grip on her legs. First one began to move, then the other.

There was a tremendous gurgle, then a hiss and with one final heave Tracy and Belinda pulled Holly free.

All three lay face down, panting.

Holly was the first to get to her feet. She looked down at herself in horror. Her jeans and trainers were covered in thick, black mud.

'Talk about the creature from the black lagoon,' she said with a wry grin. 'Mum's going to be furious. These are my best jeans.' She held up one leg. 'And look at my trainers! They'll never be the same again!'

Belinda scrambled to her feet. 'You can sling them in the washing machine when we get back. Come on, or we're never going to get there.'

But after another half hour wandering on the moor, they had to admit they were hopelessly lost.

They sat down on a rock and studied the map.

'What's that?' Belinda pointed to a black dot.

'It's a shepherd's hut,' said Holly frowning. She didn't like to admit she had absolutely no idea where they were.

'I saw that just back there,' said Tracy, pointing the way they had just come. 'I reckon we've been going round in circles.'

Holly hit her playfully on the head with the map. 'Why didn't you say so?'

'I just did!' Tracy said indignantly.

Holly grinned and pointed to another mark. 'Well, there you are then, you two. There it is – Hill Beck Farm.'

Ahead, the mist was beginning to lift. Tracy jumped up. 'Race you!'

Belinda groaned.

Holly took one more look at the map. There was the road from Willow Dale, the hill, the beck and, now she looked, even the top of the hill with drawings of long grass to indicate a boggy area.

Beside her, Belinda was pointing to the map. 'What's that symbol there?'

Holly turned the map over, frowning. 'According to the key, it's a deep gorge.' She stared at Belinda. 'Oh, no, it's right where Tracy's heading!' She leaped to her feet. 'Tracy, wait!'

But Tracy had gone, sprinting off into the mist. '*Traa-c-c-y!*' Holly's voice shouted into nothingness.

Belinda jumped up. 'We'd better get after her!'

By the time they reached her, Tracy was standing over the edge of the gully looking dazed.

'Are you all right?' Holly gasped as she ran up behind her.

Tracy turned with a bright smile. 'Sure, no problem, Ace Navigator. There must be some way of getting across.'

'If you're a kangaroo,' Belinda remarked drily.

'There's a bridge just up there,' said Holly. 'I was just going to tell you that when you hared off like a greyhound.'

Across the bridge, the mist finally rolled away. The dale was bathed in sunlight. And there in front, down in the valley, was a cluster of tumbledown buildings.

The three friends stood on the ridge looking at it.

'Hill Beck Farm,' said Holly, feeling pleased with herself. Her navigating hadn't been brilliant but they'd got here in the end.

'Yippee!' yelled Tracy and began running down the hill.

'Won't she ever learn?' Holly said with a grin. 'Come on, Belinda. Let's see if we can find Meltdown!'

12 Peril at Hill Beck Farm

Hill Beck Farm was no more than a cluster of corrugated iron buildings, sadly neglected. Sheds leaned at crazy angles; a cobbled yard was thick with grass and weeds. One wall of a stone building with a black tiled roof had collapsed. It looked as if it had once been a house. A high, wire mesh fence had been put up round the perimeter. There was a large wooden notice by the gate. 'Danger – Keep Out' it warned in red letters.

'Not exactly the place to keep horses, is it?' said Belinda disappointedly. They arrived at the bottom of the slope and stood wondering where to begin searching for Meltdown. 'I mean, how would you get them up here for a start?' she added.

'Look,' said Holly. 'There *was* a road once and it looks as if someone's driven a lorry up here quite recently.' She went across to examine deep tyre marks in the mud. The other two followed.

They stared at one another.

'Jack Pierce,' they all said at once.

Belinda looked round wildly. 'But where's Melt-down?' she cried. 'You don't think he's locked him up in one of these horrible places? Poor baby!'

'Well, I'm going to look,' said Tracy, climbing the gate. 'We haven't trekked all the way here for nothing.'

She left the others clambering over.

'Be careful,' called Holly. She turned to Belinda. 'You go round that way. And I'll look over here, OK?'

'OK,' Belinda said. 'I'll shout if I find anything.'

Holly headed off in the direction of a tall, corru-gated iron shed.

As she got nearer, the grass was almost waist high. There were piles of scrap metal, rusted and falling to bits. In places, the ground dipped suddenly, then rose up again as if there were things buried just below the surface. She could see Tracy peering cautiously into the old house. Belinda was sitting on a tussock of grass, cleaning her glasses on the sleeve of her sweat-shirt.

As Holly turned to go back, the ground seemed to open up beneath her feet. She threw out her arms wildly trying to clutch on to something, anything. Clods of earth, clumps of grass came away in her hands as she desperately tried to stop herself falling. But it was no use. Holly was plunging downwards through a hole in the ground.

For one horrible moment she thought she'd

never reach the bottom. She screamed, clutching madly at the sides. Her fingernails snagged as she grabbed frantically at protruding tree roots and rocks embedded in the earth. She screamed again but the sound was lost.

Then suddenly there was nothing, only the noise of tumbling stones and debris and a sickening thud as she hit the ground.

Inside one of the abandoned buildings, Tracy had made a discovery.

'Belinda!' she called urgently. 'Over here!'

Belinda came out of one of the sheds and ran over. Tracy was pointing to a fresh pile of hay. Beside it, a pitchfork was propped up against the wall.

'That means Meltdown's got to be here some-where,' said Belinda. 'But I've looked everywhere and there's no sign of him. It's hopeless, Tracy. We may as well go home.'

'Come on, Belinda, cheer up,' said Tracy. 'We'll find him, I know we will. Let's see if Holly's had any luck, huh?'

They were just going back outside when Tracy stopped. She grabbed Belinda's arm. 'Oh, lordy, I don't believe it!'

The sound of a truck's engine met their ears. They could just see it, trundling along the old road towards Hill Beck Farm.

'Quick!' Tracy pulled Belinda back inside the shed. 'Under here!'

They scrambled under the pile of hay, pulling handfuls over the top of them. They lay still, scared even to breathe. Dust filled Belinda's nose and she sneezed violently.

'Shh!' Tracy snapped. She could only hope that Holly had heard the lorry coming and had got out of sight as well.

The lorry trundled on towards Hill Beck Farm, lurching and bouncing on the rutted road. It pullled up in the gateway. Jack Pierce got out and stretched.

Tracy raised her head. Through the crooked doorway of the shed she saw him bend down to look at something on the ground.

'What's he doing?' Belinda whispered.

'I'm not sure,' Tracy lifted her head a bit higher. 'He's found something by the gate.' She saw Jack Pierce stand up again and look round the yard with a frown. Suddenly, Tracy realised what he had seen.

She crouched down again and whispered in Belinda's ear. 'I think he's seen our footprints in the mud.'

'Oh, no!' exclaimed Belinda. 'Now what are we going to do?'

Tracy could just see the truck parked by the closed gate. Jack Pierce had disappeared inside one of the other buildings.

'Keep our heads down!' Tracy said, diving back under the hay. 'He's gone over to the other side. Maybe that's where Meltdown is.'

But Jack Pierce had come out again and was heading their way.

They lay flat on their faces, hearts thudding with fear. Jack Pierce had entered the shed. Tracy's fists were clenched. If he discovered them now, lord knows what he'd do with them!

He stood in the doorway, looking round. Then, to their horror, they heard the screech of metal prongs against stone as he picked up the pitchfork. He began stabbing wildly at the hay.

Tracy almost screamed out loud as the vicious spikes landed centimetres from her nose. She bit her lip to stop herself from crying out.

Pierce raised the fork again and thrust it down. The sharp points hit the stone floor beneath with a clang. The next time it came down close to Belinda's face. Her breath hissed through her teeth but she didn't move a muscle. One cry, one movement, would give them away for sure.

Pierce swore and gave one last thrust into the hay. This time, the fork went right through the sleeve of Belinda's sweatshirt. She screwed her eyes up tightly. She was lucky it hadn't gone right through *her*!

The man swore again and threw the pitchfork

down angrily. He strode outside and stood with his hands on his hips. Then he turned and stomped across the yard.

After a few minutes, Tracy slowly lifted her head and peered out. Pierce had disappeared. There was the sound of a door slamming and the truck's engine suddenly came to life.

Tracy waited a while then got to her knees. 'It's OK. I think he's going. You stay here and I'll go look.'

Belinda sat up and picked bits of straw from behind her glasses. 'For goodness sake, be careful, Tracy!'

Tracy crawled to the doorway and peered out. The truck had gone. There was no sign of Jack Pierce, or, thank goodness, of Holly. She'd had the good sense to stay hidden until he'd gone.

Then Tracy noticed the gate was open and there were new deep ruts leading into the yard. Pierce hadn't gone at all. He had driven the truck *through* the gate and parked it beside one of the sheds. As she turned to warn Belinda, an arm came round the corner and grabbed her by the throat. Jack Pierce had tricked them!

'Get off!' Tracy kicked and struggled. But it was no good. He had a grip like iron.

'You let her go!' Belinda ran forward and kicked his leg. Then she fell back with a gasp. In his hand Pierce held the stun gun.

His face split into what almost passed for a smile.

'That fooled you, didn't it? Right, you two,' he said. 'I've just about had enough of you trespassing on my property.' He gave Tracy a shove towards a small building with a wooden door. With his free hand he pulled a bunch of baler twine from his pocket. 'OK,' he said, pushing her again. 'In there.' He grabbed Belinda's arm and pulled her along. 'You too, fatty.'

By the door he made them stop. He handed Belinda a length of twine. 'Now tie your friend up,' he commanded.

'But— ' Belinda spluttered.

'Just do it!' He waved the gun menacingly. 'This works just as well on people as it does on animals,' he threatened. 'Put your hands behind you,' he told Tracy. He gave Belinda another push. 'And make sure you tie them tight!'

When Belinda finished binding Tracy's hands, he checked the twine was secure and pushed Tracy inside. He took another length of twine and tied Belinda's hands in front of her, pulling it as tight as he could. Belinda winced and struggled but it was no good. He soon had her trussed up like a turkey. He shoved her in with Tracy and slammed the door. They heard the sound of a key turning in the lock.

Then there was silence.

Tracy was sitting on an old, wooden toilet seat.

'A great place to spend your holiday,' Belinda stood with her back against the door. 'An ancient outside loo!'

There was hardly room to move. Light filtered through the gap at the bottom of the door and through the three round holes cut near the top. Belinda stood on tiptoe and peered out through one of the holes.

'I can't see Holly,' she said. 'I bet she's been watching.'

Tracy was struggling to get her hands free. 'I sure hope so. She'll have to come up with a way of getting us out of here. This place wasn't designed for two people. Especially if one of them's your size, Belinda.'

Belinda looked hurt. 'Hey, just because that horrible man called me "fatty". Surely I'm not *that* big, am I?'

Tracy grinned. 'Well, let's just say you're large.'

Belinda sniffed. 'I can't help it if I've got a healthy appetite.'

Tracy was still struggling with her bonds. 'Well, if Holly doesn't turn up soon you could be a lot thinner by the time we get out.'

'We should have saved some sandwiches,' said Belinda.

'Yeah,' agreed Tracy. 'It's a wonderful place for a picnic!'

Belinda peered through the holes again. 'Hey, he's really going this time!' The truck had reversed out of the gateway and was trundling off down the track. She turned to Tracy with a grin. 'He's going to be mad as anything when he finds out Holly's been here all the time.'

It was only after about ten minutes they began to realise Holly wasn't coming to rescue them after all.

'Where *is* that girl?' Tracy said impatiently.

They shouted Holly's name over and over but she still didn't appear.

Belinda looked worried. 'What on earth's happened to her?'

Tracy shrugged. 'I don't know, but it looks like we've got to try to get out of here ourselves.' She struggled with her bonds again. The twine was rubbing her wrists raw. 'Hey, Belinda, try to get these off.'

'And how do you propose I do that?' Belinda said.

'I'll turn round and you try to undo them.'

Tracy managed to shuffle round until she had her back to Belinda. Belinda winced as she fiddled with the string. It was no easy task trying to undo knots when your own hands were tied together. 'It's no good,' she said, perspiration breaking out on her forehead. 'What we need are a few lessons from Houdini!'

'Yeah, well there's no room for him in here!' Tracy exclaimed.

Above their heads, the old iron cistern was crumbling with rust. Belinda looked up. 'Hey, if I stood on the seat maybe I could rub the string on the corner. It looks pretty sharp!'

It was worth a try. Tracy moved to one side. Belinda clambered clumsily up on the seat. Her arms ached as she rubbed the twine against the rough iron, to and fro, to and fro. She groaned. 'My arms are falling off!' She stopped and leaned against the wall, her face flushed with effort.

But Tracy could see the twine was beginning to fray. 'Just a few more times,' she encouraged. 'It's going to work!'

Sure enough, after a few more rubs, the string frayed and broke. Belinda jumped down, rubbing her wrists. 'Right!' she said. 'Let's have another go at yours.'

In minutes Tracy's hands were free. She shrugged off the rucksack and ran her hand through her hair. 'Who needs Houdini?' she grinned. 'Now, all we've got to do is break down the door!'

'Great,' said Belinda. 'Is *that* all?'

'It should be easy,' Tracy said, putting her shoulder to it. 'It looks pretty rotten to me.' Tracy pushed as hard as she could but the door didn't give at all. She tried again, grunting with effort. She ran her hands through her hair. 'It's no good – it won't budge.' She bent and looked through the keyhole. 'The key's still in the lock,' she said.

'Fat lot of good that is,' said Belinda.

Tracy looked thoughtful. 'If we could just get hold of it . . .'

Belinda was fanning herself with the map. She stopped suddenly. 'Hey,' she said, her eyes gleaming. She opened it up. 'If we could poke this map under the door and then push the key out from this side . . .'

Tracy's face lit up, '. . . and get it to land on the paper, we could pull it back through!' She was already looking around for something to push through the keyhole. Suddenly her face lit up. 'I know.' She wrenched her camera case from her bag. 'I always keep a pen handy.' She held up a slender gold pen. 'Kurt gave me this for my birthday.'

'Excellent!' Belinda knelt down and slid the map under the door. 'That should be far enough.'

Tracy poked the pen into the keyhole. She twiddled it around then pushed. They heard a thud as the key fell out the other side.

Belinda gritted her teeth. Very carefully she pulled the map towards her.

'Oh, please,' Tracy said. 'Please let it be on there!'

13 Devising a plan

Holly pushed back her hair and sat up with a groan. She struggled to her feet. The breath had been knocked from her lungs and she felt bruised all over. Her hands were scratched and sore.

Where on earth was she? It was gloomy, practically dark. The only light came from the hole she had plunged through. Holly looked up and caught a glimpse of sky way above her head. But the sides of the shaft were sheer. *Well*, she thought grimly, *I won't be able to get out the way I got in.*

As her eyes got used to the gloom, Holly saw she was in a passage of some kind. Suddenly she noticed a tiny glimmer of light at the end. With a bit of luck it was the way out.

Holly began groping her way along the tunnel. The ground was strewn with fallen rocks and, further on, boulders were piled almost to the roof. The glimmer of light was shining through a tiny gap to one side.

Holly's heart thumped painfully in her chest. She had to get out. Tracy and Belinda would be frantic with worry. Maybe if she yelled they would hear her.

'Tracy!' Holly shouted as loudly as she could. 'Belinda!' Her voice echoed round the passage and bounced back at her.

She stood holding her breath.

'Tracy!' she yelled again. *'Belinda!'*

Holly almost panicked. What if they never found her? She could be walled up in here for ever! There was only one thing to do. She had to move the stones and make a hole big enough to crawl through.

She began heaving them aside, ignoring the pain of her sore fingers. Sweating, she lifted them away one by one until at last there was a gap just large enough to crawl through. Head first, Holly squeezed into the opening. She heaved herself through, panting with effort. But she was getting nowhere. She was stuck fast!

'Oh, no!' she gasped, wriggling her body frantically. She took a deep breath and with one final heave she was through. She put out her arms and lay flat on the ground, gasping for breath. She got to her feet and looked around.

In the distance, light streamed through the tunnel entrance.

'Thank goodness!' Holly ran forward. She almost tripped as her feet came into contact with something hard. Looking down, she saw it was a small iron railway track leading down towards the tunnel entrance. A bit further on, a little metal truck lay tipped over on its side. Next to it were a couple of old shovels and a pickaxe.

It suddenly dawned on her what kind of place she was in. 'It's an old mine!' Holly said to herself. No wonder that bus driver had said the place had caved in. And no wonder she had fallen through a hole. The place had subsided, and that's why the Pierce family had moved out!

She hurried along, following the track. Eventually she burst out of the tunnel entrance into daylight.

She took a deep breath. 'Belinda! Tracy! Where are you?'

There was no sign of them anywhere. Next to the tunnel entrance someone had rigged up a makeshift door of corrugated iron. It looked as if there had once been two tunnels side by side. There were a few more old tools scattered about. A pick and shovel and a couple of crow-bars lay in a heap by the entrance.

Behind the door, Holly heard a soft whinny and the thud of hooves on the ground. She peered in through a gap beside the hinges. There were two horses inside. One was the grey mare Holly had seen being loaded into the truck that day at Snowdrop Farm. The other one was Meltdown.

Holly's heart leaped with excitement. She could have shouted with joy!

'Belinda, Tracy – I've found them!' Holly gave a great whoop of delight and ran into the centre of the yard expecting her friends to appear from one of the buildings. When there was no sign of them she ran back to the horses.

'Don't worry, Meltdown,' she called through the door. 'We'll soon get you out.' She peered through the gap again. Then Holly noticed some-one had just put down fresh hay and the horses were munching great mouthfuls. Holly gasped. Someone had been here recently, maybe even while she was groping her way out of the tun-nel.

Then Holly saw fresh tyre marks in the mud by the gate. They definitely hadn't been there when the three of them arrived.

Holly whirled round. 'Belinda! Tracy! Where *are* you?'

But there was no sign of them. The place looked as deserted as a ghost town. Surely they hadn't gone home without her. Unless – Holly froze. Had Jack Pierce arrived and discovered Belinda and Tracy poking around his property?

Holly cupped her hands round her mouth and shouted again.

At last, Tracy and Belinda appeared from behind the old house. Bits of hay were sticking out of

Belinda's hair and Tracy looked as if she'd been dragged through a hedge backwards.

They gazed at one another in surprise.

'Holly!' Belinda exclaimed, staring at Holly's torn jeans, scratched hands and face covered in mud. 'Where on earth have you been? We've been shouting like mad!'

'I fell down a hole,' Holly told her. 'What happened to *you*? I've been yelling as well!'

'We got locked in the loo!' Tracy and Belinda chorused. They all burst out laughing.

When they sobered up, Belinda explained how Jack Pierce had tricked them.

'And we thought you'd be watching and would come to get us out,' said Tracy. 'We were really worried when you didn't turn up.'

'And I thought you'd gone back without me,' cried Holly.

'As if we would!' exclaimed Belinda.

'Well,' said Holly, 'the *good* news is that I've found Meltdown!'

Belinda's face lit up. 'Where?'

'Come on, I'll show you.'

Holly led the way to the tunnel entrance where Meltdown and the grey horse were imprisoned.

'We've got to get them out.' Belinda looked in horror at the heavy padlock on the door. She rattled it. 'Meltdown, baby, I'm going to get you out of there.'

161

Tracy stood with her hands on her hips. 'I sure don't know how.'

They looked around for something to smash the lock. Tracy picked up a crow-bar but even after repeated hammerings the lock wouldn't budge.

'Let's have a go.' Belinda tried but had no luck. She looked ready to burst into tears. 'All this way,' she wailed, 'and we can't get him out.'

'I've got an idea.' Holly ran to get a pickaxe she had seen in the tunnel entrance.

'Great!' said Belinda. 'That'll do the trick!'

Holly swung the axe high and brought it down with a resounding clang against the padlock. The lock shuddered but didn't break.

'Let me try!' Tracy took it from Holly's hands. She swung it high, hitting the lock with all the strength she could muster. It bounced but stayed firmly attached to the door.

'It's no good,' she panted. 'I can't shift it.'

'There's only one thing we can do,' said Holly. 'We'll have to fetch help.'

'There's no way I'm leaving Meltdown here,' said Belinda stubbornly.

Holly took her arm. 'Look, Belinda. He's not in any danger. A little while longer won't hurt.'

'But Jack Pierce could ship him off anywhere he likes,' Belinda wailed. Her eyes brimmed with tears.

Holly shook her head. 'No, he's planning to steal

162

another one, remember? He won't take Meltdown away yet.'

'OK,' Belinda agreed reluctantly. 'At least we've got enough evidence now to get Jack Pierce locked up.'

Tracy looked thoughtful. 'Have we?' she said. 'He could just deny bringing Meltdown here. Just because the horses are on his property it doesn't mean to say he stole them himself, does it? He could just say someone dumped them here without his knowledge.'

'But it's pretty obvious,' protested Belinda.

'The police will still have to prove it,' said Holly. She frowned. 'What we really need is a confession.'

'That's not very likely,' Tracy piped up.

'Well, OK then,' Holly said. 'We've got to trap him into it and make sure the police are there when we do it.'

'And just how do we do that?' said Belinda.

Holly chewed her lip. 'We need to get Grant and Jack Pierce together.'

'Maybe we could trick them into saying something they'll regret,' suggested Tracy.

'Hmm,' said Belinda thoughtfully. 'We know Grant's going to be at the horse show. Perhaps we could get Jack Pierce to go too?'

'Yes,' said Holly. Her mind raced. She remembered how sorry Fran was when she'd told Holly

163

that Grant had been in some kind of trouble. Maybe she regretted telling Jack Pierce as well? She admitted that sometimes she said too much. This might just be her chance to make amends.

'I wonder if Fran would help?' Holly blurted.

'Fran?' exclaimed Belinda. 'But we think she was the one who told Jack about Grant in the first place.'

'I know,' said Holly. 'But I got the feeling she'd really regretted it and that things had sort of spun out of control. I think I'll go and ask her. If she won't help then we'll have to think of something else.'

By the time they got back to Belinda's the whole plan had been hatched. They decided to get started right away.

'I'll ring Fran from home tonight,' Holly said as her dad came to take her home. 'Let's meet at Annie's Tea-room in the morning and I'll let you know what she says.'

'OK,' said Belinda. 'And if she does agree to help, I'll ring Mrs Maylam, tell her we've found her horse and ask if she'll help us too.'

'And then we'd better go and see Sergeant Hadcroft,' said Tracy. 'I sure hope she'll go along with our plan.' She bit her lip. 'If she won't, then I don't know what's going to happen to poor old Meltdown!'

*   *   *

Holly turned up at Annie's Tea-room next morning full of excitement. Tracy was already there with Kurt. She had bumped into him on the way there. Kurt was chatting about bowling techniques. Tracy was only half listening. She couldn't concentrate on anything but the plans for the following day.

The doorbell clanged and Holly came in. She got a Coke from the woman behind the counter and sat down beside Tracy.

Kurt rose. 'Sorry, folks,' he said with a grin. 'I've got to run. I'm going to the show tomorrow to take some pictures and I've got to get a film. I don't suppose Belinda will want to go without a horse, will she?'

Tracy shrugged. 'She might want to go along just to watch.'

Kurt bent to kiss her goodbye. 'OK. If you go with her I'll see you there.'

Holly felt relieved. Tracy obviously hadn't told Kurt what they were up to. The fewer people who knew, the better.

When Kurt had gone Tracy leaned forward eagerly. 'How did you get on when you called Fran?'

'Fine,' Holly said excitedly. 'She's meeting us here at eleven o'clock.'

Tracy's eyes shone. 'Great. What did you say?'

'I said we needed her help and that it was something that would help Grant.'

'Help him!' Tracy exclaimed. She sucked the last of her milkshake up through the straw.

'Yes,' said Holly. 'Grant obviously knows about the horse thefts even though he refused to have anything to do with them. He *could* be accused of withholding evidence. If the police knew Pierce was threatening him, he might not get prosecuted.'

Tracy nodded. 'Yeah, I guess that's true. But it won't stop the bookmaker taking him to court, will it?'

Holly shrugged. 'No, I suppose not. That's something Grant will have to deal with himself. All *we* want is to get Belinda's horse back and the thief locked up.'

The doorbell clanged again and Belinda came in. She waved to the others then went to order an ice-cream sundae. She had mended the tear in her sleeve with black cotton.

'It'll start a new trend,' Belinda said, showing Holly and Tracy as she sat down. 'I know I've got a chest full of these at home but I like this one best.' Holly and Tracy groaned, but the look on Belinda's face when the waitress brought her sundae stopped them from teasing her further. Belinda stared at it then picked up her spoon. She toyed with it for a minute.

'What's wrong, Belinda?' said Holly. 'Don't tell me you're not hungry.'

Belinda shrugged. 'I've been thinking about Jack Pierce calling me fatty.' She looked at Holly and Tracy. 'Do you think I should go on a diet?'

Tracy shrugged. 'It's up to you.'

Belinda gazed at the glass piled high with fudge ice-cream, topped with chocolate sauce and nuts. Then she grinned and plunged her spoon into it. 'Nah! I'll start the diet tomorrow!' she said.

While she munched, Holly told Belinda that Fran had agreed to meet them. 'And did you get in touch with Jenny Maylam?' she asked Belinda anxiously.

Belinda licked her spoon. 'Yup,' she confirmed. 'She's really pleased we've found her horse. She thought our scheme to borrow Roddy was excellent. She's coming to pick me up tomorrow morning.'

'Brilliant,' said Holly. 'Now all we've got to do is persuade Fran to help us.'

As she spoke, she saw Fran outside, looking a bit lost. Holly jumped to her feet and ran to the door. She ushered Fran inside and over to their table.

'These are my friends Tracy and Belinda,' Holly said.

Fran sat down and took off her headscarf. 'How do you do,' she said.

'Would you like me to get you a drink?' Tracy asked.

Fran shook her head. 'No, thanks. Perhaps

you'd just tell me what you wanted to see me about?'

Holly did most of the explaining.

'. . . and we saw you at the market with Jack Pierce,' she concluded. 'So it's obvious you know him.'

To their horror, Fran began to cry. She fumbled in her bag and took out a handkerchief. Holly put her arm round her.

'I'm sorry,' she said. 'I didn't mean to upset you.'

Fran shook her head and blew her nose. 'I've been so stupid,' she sniffed. 'I should never have got involved with Jack Pierce.' She stared at the three friends, her dark eyes still bright with tears. 'I thought he was such a nice man,' she said, clearing her throat. 'I met him when he delivered straw for Grant's horse. I invited him in for a cup of coffee and we got talking.'

The Mystery Club leaned foward. 'How did he get to know about Grant's money problems?' asked Tracy.

'I told him,' admitted Fran. 'It was the day Grant got a summons to go to court for non-payment of debts. I was so worried, I *had* to tell someone. If the story got into the papers I knew it would ruin Grant's chances of getting into the Olympic team. The news would kill my mother!'

'Did you know Jack Pierce had stolen the horses?' asked Holly gently.

Fran sniffed and nodded. 'Yes, Jack told me he'd tried to get Grant to help him but he'd refused. He threatened to tell Mother about the court case if we told the police.'

Holly patted Fran's shoulder in sympathy. 'Look, Fran,' she said, 'if you'll help us by persuading Jack to go to the show tomorrow and our plan works, then the police will know he's been threatening Grant.'

Fran sat biting her lip. 'Yes,' she said after a moment's thought. 'I will help you. I feel really bad that I told Jack about Grant. The silly thing was, I had already decided to help my brother. I was going to sell a piece of jewellery my father left me. It would have fetched enough money to pay off the bookmakers and prevent the case coming to court. Jack Pierce persuaded me not to,' she added bitterly. 'I must have been crazy!'

'If the police *are* sympathetic towards Grant,' said Belinda, feeling sorry for Fran, 'maybe your mother need never know.'

Fran brightened up. 'Oh, I do hope so. I used to resent Grant for being so successful. I felt he'd had all the lucky breaks. But I gave up my plans to look after my mother of my own free will. No one made me do it.' Fran sighed. 'I suppose I was just taken in. Jack can be charming when he wants to be. We

169

were both lonely people and we seemed to have a lot in common.'

'We all make mistakes,' Holly said kindly.

Fran gave a wan smile. 'Yes.' She glanced at her watch then rose hastily. 'I'd better go. Mother will be getting anxious. She always worries if I'm out for too long. I'll get Jack to go to the show tomorrow, you can rely on me.' She put on her headscarf and went out.

'Right,' said Holly, when Fran had gone. Her eyes were gleaming. 'So far, so good. Now, down to the station to see Sergeant Hadcroft. Keep your fingers crossed, you two. This could be our lucky day!'

14 Tracy goes missing

The day of the Willow Dale Riding Centre show dawned bright and sunny. Belinda had no trouble in getting up. Not only was she going to see some of the best showjumpers in the county, this would be the day she got her horse back!

When the Mystery Club had told Sergeant Hadcroft of their scheme she had readily agreed to help. The police were getting nowhere with the case and anything that would speed up the arrest of the horse thief would be welcome. She had promised to meet the Mystery Club at the show at eleven o'clock, the time the senior competition would begin. If everything went according to plan she would be on hand with her tape recorder when Jack Pierce confessed. Belinda couldn't wait to see his face when she rode into the show ring on a horse that looked exactly like Meltdown!

When Belinda got downstairs she discovered her mother had already left the house. She had left a note on the kitchen table. 'Gone to the hairdresser,' it said. 'See you later.'

Belinda wolfed down a bowl of cornflakes and several slices of buttered toast and peanut butter, then went back upstairs to get dressed. Just as she was ready, a horse box arrived. Jenny Maylam from Snowdrop Farm was at the wheel.

Belinda opened the bedroom window. 'Just coming,' she shouted. She took a glance in the mirror then hurried downstairs.

Holly cycled to the riding centre. The narrow road was busy with a stream of cars and horse boxes on their way to the show. It was to be a big event this year with lots of competitions, stalls and sideshows raising money for charity. It looked as if the whole of Willow Dale would be there.

When she arrived, the place was already bustling. A cloud of steam rose from one corner of the lorry park as a blacksmith plunged his newly forged horseshoes into cold water. A couple of ponies were waiting to be shod. A man stood at the gate directing horse boxes into their positions. People wandered around looking at the brightly coloured stalls selling riding clothes and tack. Jake Barratt's voice came over the loudspeaker.

'All competitors for the novice pony class please go to ring two.'

In ring one, the junior competitors were walking the course. Holly scanned the crowd but could see no sign of Fran or Jack Pierce. In the distance she recognised Mrs Harris with her daughter, Kelly. The little girl was skipping along merrily by her mother's side. Obviously she'd made a full recovery.

Holly wandered idly round the various stalls.

'Hi, Holly. Want to buy a ticket?' Holly was surprised to see Jamie's best friend, Philip Owen, standing beside the Lucky Dip. There was a tea chest beside him with a hole cut in the top. 'It's for a good cause,' he added.

'What? The Jamie and Philip fund?' Holly grinned.

'No, Guide Dogs. We're helping my mum. She's just gone to watch the novice ponies. Go on, have a ticket, Holly.'

Holly found a ten-pence piece and handed it to Philip. 'Where's Jamie?' she asked.

'He's gone to get an ice-cream.' explained Philip.

Holly put her hand into the box and drew out a bar of chocolate. 'Thanks,' she said absently. Holly's mind wasn't really on winning a prize. She said goodbye to Philip and wandered round looking for Sergeant Hadcroft. The Mystery Club had asked her to wear plain clothes. If Jack Pierce spotted the police he might start getting suspicious.

Holly saw the sergeant at last. She was standing by the first-aid tent watching the ponies and riders file into the ring. She wore a baggy T-shirt and black leggings. The constable was with her, dressed in blue jeans and a polo shirt.

Holly heaved a sigh of relief and glanced at her

watch. Ten forty-five. It was about time Tracy turned up as well. It really wasn't like her to be late.

Holly wandered around watching the horses and riders getting warmed up. There was a feeling of excitement in the air as people took their seats around the main ring. In fifteen minutes the main event of the day would be taking place. The contest for the Riding Centre cup in which both Belinda and Grant would be taking part.

Then Holly saw Grant. He was putting Beauty through her paces in the practice ring. He looked handsome in his white jodhpurs and black riding jacket. A small ripple of applause went up from some of the stable hands as Beauty sailed effortlessly over the jumps. Grant was certainly every bit as good a rider as his mother claimed.

Holly went over to say hello. She knew she had to act normally. She didn't want to arouse his suspicions that anything was amiss.

'Hi, Holly.' Grant looked surprised to see her. He dismounted and handed Beauty's reins to one of the grooms. He removed his riding hat and wiped his brow. 'I didn't think you'd be here today.'

Holly shrugged. 'I've just come to watch.'

Grant flushed slightly. 'It's really too bad about Meltdown. The police came to see me, you know?'

'Really?' Holly feigned surprise.

174

'Yes, Belinda said I'd seen where she put the key.'

Holly shrugged. 'Oh, that's nothing. They were just eliminating you from their enquiries I expect.'

Holly noticed Grant shift his eyes rapidly away from hers. 'Yes,' he said. 'I expect you're right.'

Fran appeared, pushing Mrs D'Angelo in her wheelchair. Grant bent and kissed his mother on the cheek.

'I've come to wish you luck,' Mrs D'Angelo said to her son.

Fran drew Holly aside. 'Jack's definitely coming,' she assured Holly. 'I told him Grant wanted to see him urgently.'

'Thanks,' said Holly. 'We're really grateful for your help, Fran.'

Fran shrugged her shoulders. 'I just hope your plan doesn't backfire. What if the police arrest me and Grant?'

'I explained the circumstances to Sergeant Hadcroft,' Holly told her. 'She said she thought it would be OK. Jack Pierce has been blackmailing you both. You really didn't have any choice but to keep quiet.'

Fran gripped Holly's hand. 'Thanks,' she said warmly.

Holly made her excuses and left Grant chatting to his mother and sister. She glanced at her watch. Only ten mintues to go. She was beginning to feel anxious. Why on earth wasn't Tracy here?

Holly pushed her way through the crowd. She stopped by the first-aid tent and stood on tiptoe looking anxiously for her friend. She spied Kurt over by the refreshment stand, his camera slung round his neck. Maybe Tracy was with him?

She dashed over. 'Kurt, have you seen Tracy?' she asked quickly.

He shook his head. 'No. Is she supposed to be here?'

'Yes.' Holly bit her lip. Tracy was never late. Her pulse skipped. Maybe something had happened to her. 'I'll go and see if she's coming,' she said to Kurt. She waved goodbye and pushed her way through towards the entrance. She glanced at her watch again, her mind racing. If Tracy didn't hurry up she would miss the whole thing!

Tracy glanced at her watch as she pedalled furiously along the road to the riding centre. Just as she'd been leaving home, her father had phoned from California. It was great to talk to him and she hated to sound rushed. But by the time he hung up, she was already ten minutes late.

Tracy was about half a mile from the centre when Jack Pierce roared past in his truck. Tracy let out a whoop of delight. It looked as if things were going according to plan. She put on a spurt of energy

176

to make up for lost time. She hated being late, and Holly would already be wondering where she'd got to.

Suddenly, her bike slewed sideways and hit the verge. She slammed on the brakes and jumped off. Her front tyre was flat. She glanced frantically at her watch. It was ten minutes to eleven. It would be quicker to run the last leg of the trip than stop now to mend the puncture.

Leaving her bike in the hedge, Tracy sprinted the quarter of a mile to the riding centre. She dashed through the gate.

On the other side of the hedge she could see the crowds of people. She heard Jake's voice announcing the winners of the novice pony class. She noticed a gap in the hedge and decided to take a short cut, dodging between two lorries. But she didn't get very far. She cannoned into someone coming the other way.

'Oops!' she gasped. 'Sorry!'

Tracy found herself looking up into a pair of pale eyes with ginger eyebrows beneath the peak of a tweed cap. Jack Pierce! The last person on earth she wanted to meet.

Pierce was staring at her with a puzzled look on his face. Tracy was just about to dodge past when he grabbed her by the arm.

'What are you doing here?' he growled.

'The same as you,' Tracy retorted. She struggled

but his grip was too strong. 'I've come to see the show.'

Jack Pierce glared at her. 'How did you get away from Hill Beck?' he asked. 'Have you girls got a skeleton key or something?'

'That's for us to know and you to find out,' Tracy answered, sounding braver than she felt. She struggled again and aimed a kick at his leg. 'Let me go!' she yelled.

But there was no one around to hear. The show was in full swing and the lorry park was deserted. Everyone was watching the competitions. Tracy's mind raced. She *had* to get away.

She struggled again and tried to twist out of Pierce's grasp. But it was no good. He held her fast and began to drag her towards his truck.

'We'll see how you get on this time!' he said with a sneer. He opened the tail-gate and thrust her inside. 'I'll decide what to do with you later,' he growled. 'I've had enough of you lot interfering.' He slammed the tail-gate shut and rammed home the bolts. He strode away without looking back.

Inside the lorry, Tracy was hammering on the door.

'Let me out!' she yelled. She pounded the door again then slumped to the floor. She clenched her fist furiously and thumped the floor. Then she got up and paced around, kicking at the straw in a temper.

She ran to the door and banged on it again. 'Help!'

To her surprise, this time a voice answered. 'Hello? Who's in there?'

'I'm locked in,' she yelled. 'Can you undo the bolts? Please hurry. It's urgent!'

The voice came again. A boy's voice. A voice Tracy recognised. 'Tracy?' it said uncertainly. 'Is that you?'

15 Showdown

Behind the commentator's box, well in sight of the jumping arena, Holly was jiggling about impatiently. Only five minutes to go and there was no sign of Tracy *or* Belinda. What on earth had happened to them? She hadn't seen Jack Pierce either. Maybe he'd broken his promise to Fran and decided not to come after all.

The Mystery Club's plan seemed to be going wrong. It was all very well for Sergeant Hadcroft and her colleague to be hanging around the entrance but it looked as if they were going to be wasting their time!

Then Holly's heart skipped a beat. Jack Pierce was elbowing his way through the crowd. He was obviously looking for Grant.

'Hello, you.' A voice suddenly came at Holly's elbow. She turned swiftly.

It was Jamie, ice-cream all round his mouth.

'Oh, hi, Jamie.' Holly said vaguely. She craned her neck. Jack Pierce was standing by the ring entrance. The competitors were already lining up for the start.

'I've got something to tell you,' Jamie said.

'Not now, Jamie,' Holly said. 'Go away, will you.' Trust her little brother to turn up at the worst possible moment.

Jamie shrugged and licked his mouth. 'OK, then. I won't tell you about Tracy.'

Holly turned sharply. 'What about Tracy?'

'She's got herself locked in a truck, that's all.'

'A truck!' Holly gasped. Her mind whirled. If someone had locked Tracy inside a truck, she had a good idea who it was! She grabbed Jamie's arm. 'Where? Show me!'

'It's in the carpark. I tried to get her out but I couldn't get the bolts undone.'

'Thanks, Jamie!' Holly ran as fast as she could towards the carpark. She hadn't even had to ask Jamie what colour the truck was. It didn't take much to work out it was a blue one with *Hay and Straw Merchant* written on the side.

As Holly ran, she glanced at her watch. Only minutes to go! *Belinda, where on earth are you?*

Holly soon found the truck. She jumped up on the bumper and wrestled the bolts undone. Tracy bounded out.

'What happened?' Holly panted.

'I'll tell you later,' Tracy said quickly. 'It's time for Belinda's competition. Come on!'

181

'Tracy!'

But Tracy had gone speeding through the gate and racing towards the main ring. Holly was hot on her heels.

Tracy managed to push her way quickly through the crowd towards the entrance to the ring. She came to a halt behind the two police officers.

Grant was just finishing his round. There was a murmur of sympathy from the spectators as Beauty's hind legs just clipped the top rail of the last fence and it tumbled off. Up until then, his performance had been perfect.

'Four faults,' Jake announced as Grant left the ring to loud applause.

'Belinda's next!' Tracy whispered as Holly appeared beside her.

'But that's what I'm trying to tell you, you idiot,' Holly panted. 'Belinda's not here!'

Tracy spun round. 'What?' Her eyes widened in disbelief. 'Not here? Where is she?'

Holly shrugged. 'That's just it, I don't know!'

Jack Pierce was waiting as Grant dismounted. Grant looked away as Jack spoke to him. Then he shrugged and shook his head. Jack Pierce frowned and looked confused.

Sergeant Hadcroft and the constable were standing within ear-shot. The sergeant had her small tape recorder in her hand, ready to switch it on.

Jake's voice came over the loudspeaker again.

'Next competitor, Number two. Belinda Hayes on Meltdown.'

A murmur went through the crowd. Then there was silence. Everyone looked at the entrance expectantly.

At the announcement, Jack Pierce looked up sharply. He said something to Grant. Grant shrugged again.

Holly and Tracy held their breath.

Tracy ran her hands through her hair. 'Where has that girl got to?'

Holly's heart thudded a message of desperation. She wrung her hands together. It was OK for her and Tracy to be here but unless Belinda turned up the whole plan would go to pot!

'It's no good,' Tracy said looking crestfallen. 'Everything's gone wrong – she's not coming.'

'I'm sorry,' Jake's voice boomed once more. 'We don't seem to have . . .'

Suddenly, Holly grabbed Tracy's arm. Above the heads of the crowd she had seen the unmistakable figure of Belinda on horseback. She was trotting smartly towards the main ring. Holly jumped with excitement. 'There she is!'

Jack Pierce stared in disbelief as Belinda trotted past and into the ring on a bold, chestnut thoroughbred. She was dressed in her black riding jacket and spotless beige jodhpurs, her hair tied neatly back under her riding hat. She gave Pierce a triumphant look as she swept past. Spying Holly and Tracy she gave them a cheery wave.

Jack Pierce's face grew scarlet with rage. He turned furiously to Grant. His eyes narrowed. 'It was you, wasn't it?' he bellowed. 'You went up to Hill Beck and let those kids out. You fetched that darned horse down just so she could ride it in the competition. I might have known you wouldn't be able to keep your mouth shut!'

Grant was trying to get a word in, but nothing would stop Jack now he was in full swing. 'You wait until I tell your mother all about the court case,' he stormed. 'She'll probably have a heart attack. And as for that sister of yours, she's nothing but a pathetic . . .'

Grant looked dumbstruck. He just stood there listening while Pierce went on with his torrent of abuse.

Holly could see Sergeant Hadcroft listening eagerly and recording Pierce's every word. Their plan had been brilliant!

In the ring, Belinda and Jenny Maylam's chestnut thoroughbred, Roddy, were jumping a faultless round. Only an expert on horses could have known Belinda's mount was not Meltdown.

Tracy was clutching Holly's arm, her hand over her mouth trying to stifle her laughter as Jack Pierce went on shouting at Grant. 'He's digging himself deeper and deeper!' she chortled.

When the sergeant had heard enough she tucked the tape recorder into her pocket and nodded to the constable.

They both stepped forward. The sergeant put her hand on Jack's arm.

'Jack Pierce?' she said.

Pierce spun round. 'Yes?' he snapped.

The sergeant produced her warrant. 'I'm arresting you in connection with the recent theft of two horses.'

Suddenly Jack Pierce saw Holly and Tracy standing behind the officers. A look of realisation dawned on his face. He spun round, wrenching his arm from the sergeant's grasp. The constable lunged forward but Pierce had gone, elbowing his way rapidly through the crowd. Holly craned her neck. 'Stop that man!' she shouted desperately.

Tracy was already pushing her way through after him. Holly dodged down under the fence and raced across the corner of the ring. She thrust through the gate. Maybe she could head him off.

There was no sign of the police officers, or of Tracy. People seemed to hinder her at every turn. She almost fell over a woman with a push-chair, and a toddler almost went sprawling as Holly tried to get past. Apologising, Holly lunged forward again, dodging this way and that, elbowing through the throng.

Holly jumped up and caught a glimpse of Pierce's

tweed cap disappearing in the direction of the lorry park. Her heart thudded with anxiety. He was getting away! Jack Pierce was getting away!

At last, Holly was out in the open. She spurted after him. There was still no sign of Tracy or the police. Then she spotted Pierce heading for his truck. Holly groaned. She'd never catch him now!

Suddenly, there was the thud of horse's hooves behind her. Holly spun round. A figure on horseback had emerged from the crowd and was heading towards her. It was Belinda.

'Belinda!' Holly yelled, jumping up and down. 'Quick, he's getting away!'

Belinda kicked her mount into a fast gallop. Turf flew in all directions as horse and rider thundered towards the fleeing man. As she caught up with him, Belinda leaned down and grabbed at his collar. Pierce went flying. Holly heard him cry out as he tumbled headlong.

Belinda's horse skidded to a halt. She swung her leg over the saddle, jumped down and dashed back. Jack Pierce was still lying face down on the grass, his breath knocked from his body. Belinda plonked herself down on top of him. He tried to struggle to his feet but with Belinda on his back he couldn't move.

'Gotcha!' Belinda cried triumphantly.

After that, everyone arrived at once. Tracy rushed up, the sergeant and constable in her wake.

Tracy was grinning from ear to ear. 'Brilliant, Belinda!' she cried, clapping her hands.

'Well done!' Sergeant Hadcroft said, looking flushed. 'We couldn't get through the crowd.'

Belinda stood up. 'He's all yours,' she said with a broad smile. 'And you're welcome to him!'

The police officers took Pierce by the arms and hauled him to his feet. They marched him off to their car parked in the stable yard.

Holly and Tracy gave Belinda a pat on the back. 'That was absolutely great, Belinda!' Holly exclaimed. Better than a Wild West show. But where on earth *were* you? We thought you weren't coming!'

'Roddy cast a shoe as we were getting him out of the box,' Belinda explained. 'We had to wait for the blacksmith.'

By now, Jenny Maylam had come to collect her horse. Belinda handed over the reins. 'Thanks for lending him to us.' She gave Roddy a pat on the rump. 'He's great. In fact so great we came first in the competition!'

Jenny Maylam smiled. 'I knew Roddy wouldn't let you down. And it certainly looks as if he fooled Jack Pierce.'

'He certainly did,' the Mystery Club chorused.

'Right,' said Belinda. 'Now we've got to go and get Meltdown and your grey mare, Jenny.'

'I'll put Roddy into a stable and we'll go right now,' the young woman replied.

In the stable yard, the sergeant was talking to the D'Angelos. Fran called them over.

'We've told our mother everything,' she said. 'She's taken it very well; haven't you, mother?'

Mrs D'Angelo nodded. 'My son's been very foolish,' she said. 'If he'd told me about his debts in the first place this would never have happened.'

'I know that now,' Grant said. 'And I'm really sorry.' He turned to the Mystery Club. 'The sergeant said things might not go too badly for us, and we've got you three to thank for it.'

Mrs D'Angelo smiled at the three friends. 'I'm going to pay off Grant's debts,' she said. 'And hopefully the police won't prosecute Grant and Fran for withholding information.' She looked up at Grant and took his hand. 'I really don't think this will affect his chance of getting into the Olympic team next year.'

Sergeant Hadcroft came over to speak to them. 'Thanks, you three. We've got enough evidence to lock Jack Pierce up for a very long time.'

'Good!' the three friends chorused.

'What are you going to do now?' the sergeant asked.

'We're going to get Meltdown,' said Belinda. She strode over to the police car and wrenched open the door. She held out her hand. 'The key, please,' she said to Jack Pierce.

Jack Pierce scowled and handed over the key to Meltdown's hiding-place without protest.

Half an hour later, Miss Maylam's horse box was trundling up the rough road to Hill Beck Farm.

In the cab, Belinda was jiggling up and down in her seat excitedly. 'Oh, my baby,' she cried. 'I can't wait to see him again!'

The lorry drew to a halt and she leaped out. She thrust open the gate and ran over to the old tunnel entrance. 'I'm here, Meltdown,' she shouted, thrusting the key into the lock. 'I've come to rescue you!' She wrenched off the padlock and pulled the door open wide. She ran inside and threw her arms round her beloved thoroughbred's neck. 'Meltdown, baby,' she cried. 'Are you OK?'

Holly and Tracy were waiting as Belinda led her horse out into the open.

She looked at the others, her eyes sparkling with tears. 'Look at him. Isn't he wonderful?'

'Yes, wonderful,' Holly and Tracy agreed, nodding their heads.

Belinda rubbed her hands together. 'Right!' she said. 'We'll take Meltdown home then we'll go to Annie's for a huge sundae to celebrate, OK?'

'What about your diet?' said Tracy. 'You were supposed to be starting it today.'

189

'Oh, never mind about that,' said Belinda. 'If we're going to do this kind of thing regularly, I need to keep up my strength!'

Holly and Tracy chuckled. It was great to see Belinda her old self again.

Chatting amiably, they helped Belinda and Jenny Maylam put the horses into the lorry. As they drove home, the sun cast a bright light over the moorland in front.

Holly sat back in the seat with a sigh of contentment. What a good feeling it was to be here with her friends. They certainly made a great team. Holly, Tracy and Belinda – the Mystery Club.

DECEPTIONS

by Fiona Kelly

Holly, Belinda and Tracy are back in the
twelth thrilling adventure in the
Mystery Club series, published by
Knight Books.

Here is the first chapter . . .

1 A Secret Meeting

'Jamie! Are you deaf?' Holly shouted. 'The phone's ringing!'

Normally Holly would do anything to get to the phone before Jamie. The last thing she wanted was him speaking to her friends. Especially Tracy and Belinda. They had much more important things to talk about. That's why Holly liked to get to the phone first. But just at the moment she was stuck in her bedroom.

'Jamie!' She tried again. Still no answer. *Typical!* she thought.

Holly began scrambling over piles of books. She had chosen the first morning of the holidays to rearrange her vast collection of mystery novels.

Holly reached the door and swept the books that were blocking the way into a jumbled heap. The next moment she was racing down the stairs. As she reached the final step, the door to the sitting-room opened and Jamie shot out.

He grabbed the receiver. 'The Adams household. Jamie Adams speaking,' he said in a stupid voice.

Holly groaned with embarrassment and tried to take the receiver from him. But Jamie pulled a face and turned his back on her.

'Yeah!' he said. 'Yeah . . . of course!' And finally, 'Wait a minute.'

Jamie passed the receiver over his shoulder. 'It's for you,' he told Holly.

'Who is it?' she whispered.

Jamie shrugged. 'I dunno. Vijay Jempson I think', he called out as he disappeared into the sitting-room and slammed the door behind him.

Holly was puzzled. She'd never heard of Vijay Jempson. 'Sorry to keep you waiting,' she said into the phone. 'This is Holly Adams.'

'At last!' It was a woman's voice and she sounded irritated. 'I was beginning to think I'd got the wrong number. This is P.J. Benson.'

Holly froze.

'Are you still there?' said the woman.

Holly took a deep breath. 'I'm still here,' she said. 'Who did you say it was?'

'Benson. P.J. Benson. You wrote to me. Don't you remember?'

Holly certainly did remember. How could she forget? P.J. Benson was her favourite author. She wrote the kind of mysteries that had more twists in them than a bowl of spaghetti.

'So, do you remember or not?'

'Oh yes.' Holly gasped. In the letter she had

told the author all about the Mystery Club and about some of the adventures the friends had had together. She'd also asked if the writer would agree to be interviewed for *Winformation*, the school magazine.

'Well,' the woman continued, 'it so happens that I'm living near Willow Dale for a few months while I work on my next book. I thought we might meet up.'

Holly couldn't believe her ears. 'I'd love to!' she said. 'Where are you living?'

'That doesn't matter,' the writer answered. 'I keep my business and private lives quite separate. There's a hotel in Willow Dale called the the Queen's Head. We can meet there. This afternoon. Four o'clock. Can you make it?'

'Four? I think so.'

'Good. And, Holly, I value my privacy very much indeed. I don't want anyone else to know I'm in the area. So please don't tell anyone about our meeting. Don't even say you've spoken to me. If you do there'll be no interview. Do you understand?'

'Yes.'

'Fine! Four o'clock then.' And the phone went dead.

Holly stared dumbly at the receiver. She could hardly believe what was happening. Not only had she just spoken to P.J. Benson, one of the greatest mystery writers of all time, but a few hours later she was actually going to *meet* her.

How would she ever keep it to herself? Especially as the Mystery Club had arranged to meet at two o'clock that afternoon at the Willon Dale ice-cream parlour.

Holly replaced the receiver and ran back upstairs. On her bedside cabinet was a brand new copy of *Fallen Angel*, P.J. Benson's latest book. Holly's mother had given it to her a few days earlier.

Holly turned the book over. On the back cover was a picture of the author. Smiling and silver-haired with a pair of round, horn-rimmed glasses, she looked like everybody's favourite aunt.

Funny, Holly thought. *She doesn't sound a bit like she looks.*

It was then that the first doubts entered Holly's mind. What if it was all a trick? The only people who knew that Holly had written to P.J. Benson were Tracy and Belinda. And they wouldn't play a joke like that on her. Would they?

Oh, well, Holly thought. *I'll soon find out. If it is them, they'll never be able to keep quiet about it.*

By the time Holly had caught the bus into Willow Dale and walked through the streets to the ice-cream parlour, she had convinced herself that the phone call from P.J. Benson was genuine. Her only worry was how to keep the secret from her two friends.

As she walked through the door, Holly could see Tracy and Belinda sitting at their favourite table. Usually Belinda would be at least five minutes late for any meeting but when ice-cream was on offer it was different.

Tracy was looking through the menu. Belinda, who looked as though she'd come straight from mucking out her horse, was already tucking in. 'C'mon over, quick,' she called as she spotted Holly. 'I've got something to tell you.'

'At least now I know how to get Belinda to turn up to meetings on time,' Holly said. 'Hold them here.'

Tracy lifted her sports bag off the spare seat so that Holly could sit down. 'Maybe we should change it from the Mystery Club to the Ice-Cream Club,' she grinned. 'We've certainly had more ice-creams than mysteries lately.'

'That's because nothing mysterious happens round here any more,' said Belinda.

'Oh, I don't know,' said Holly, almost forgetting herself for a moment.

Tracy and Belinda looked at Holly expectantly. 'What's happened?' they said together.

Holly tried to look innocent. 'Nothing,' she said.

'Is there something we don't know?' asked Tracy.

Holly shook her head. 'It's Belinda who's got the secret.'

'Me?'

'Didn't you say you had something to tell me? Sounded like it was important.'

Belinda looked blank for a moment then her eyes lit up. 'It is,' she agreed, 'very important.'

'What is it then?'

'Passion fruit and guava tastes even better with chocolate-fudge ripple, than apricot and kumquat does.'

Tracy sighed. 'This girl puts more effort into discovering the perfect combination of ice-cream than Einstein put into discovering the theory of relativity.' To the members of the Mystery Club ice-cream was a serious business. It required total concentration, so for a while no one spoke.

It was Belinda who finally broke the silence. 'Perfect!' she sighed, laying down her spoon. 'The perfect start to a holiday. A full morning's riding followed by five scoops of heaven.'

'How is Meltdown?' asked Tracy. 'Still sagging in the middle?'

Belinda looked outraged. She could stand rude comments about her weight but nobody insulted her beloved horse. 'Meltdown could carry somebody three times my weight without any problem!'

'He may have to,' said Tracy. 'If you keep eating

like this, you'll be three times your weight by the end of the holiday!'

'I've never noticed *you* refusing second helpings,' said Belinda.

'No,' agreed Tracy. 'But the difference is I'll be working the weight off at Paradise.'

'Is that where you've been this morning?' asked Holly.

'Yes,' Tracy grinned. 'It's fantastic!'

Paradise was a new health and fitness club that had just opened at Willingston, a small village just outside Willow Dale. As part of its publicity drive it had run a competition in the local paper. The prize was one month's free membership. To Tracy's delight she had won the competition.

'They've got everything there,' Tracy said. 'Swimming-pool, weights room, squash and tennis courts, even a sauna.

'Well, it's pretty obvious what you're going to be doing this holiday then,' said Holly.

'That's right,' said Tracy. 'I'm going to make the most of my month. I'll never be able to afford it after that. It's incredibly expensive. I'm planning to go there every day. By the end of this holiday I'll be so fit you won't recognise me.'

'Yes, we will,' said Belinda. 'You'll be the one with a sports bag in one hand and a triple scoop ice-cream in the other.'

'Better than having a triple scoop ice-cream in

one hand and a double scoop in the other,' Tracy laughed. 'What about you, Holly? What are you up to?'

'Well,' said Holly, 'I started off this morning by trying to rearrange my books but then—' Holly paused.

'Then what?'

'Oh, I just had to do something for my mother,' Holly ended lamely.

'You had a phone call?' asked Tracy.

'A phone call?' Suddenly Holly's suspicions flooded back. 'What do you know about a phone call?'

Tracy shrugged. 'Nothing. I just figured that if you suddenly had to do something for your mom, she must have phoned you up from work. Or is she on holiday too?'

Holly relaxed a little. 'No, she's not on holiday. I did have a phone call,' Holly agreed.

'Well, at least we sorted *that* out,' Belinda said, winking at Tracy. 'I was beginning to think something strange was going on. Now I'm getting my appetite back. So – who's for seconds?'

'We're for seconds and you're for fourths!' said Tracy.

Tracy and Belinda waved goodbye as they turned down the alley which led to the bus stop. Holly had pretended that she was going to the library but instead she set off down Market Street towards the Queen's Head Hotel.

The Queen's Head was right in the middle of the old part of Willow Dale. Holly stopped and glanced round the street to make sure no one was watching before stepping inside. Willow Dale wasn't a large town and Holly knew a lot of people.

To the left of the reception desk was a lounge. Holly headed straight for a red velvet armchair in the corner. From there she would have a good view of both the front entrance and the staircase to the upper rooms.

As she sat down, Holly half-expected Tracy and Belinda to come grinning their way towards her. But to her relief there was no sign of them at all.

Holly felt a buzz of excitement deep inside. Suddenly she was sure that this wasn't a joke. She really was going to meet her favourite author! But how would they recognise each other? P.J. Benson had no idea what Holly looked like. And Holly only had the picture on the back of the book to go by. *That 'll have to do*, she thought. *I just hope she hasn't changed much.*

The hotel was pretty quiet. Three people were sitting in the lounge and two more were talking to the reception clerk.

Holly checked her watch. It was still only five minutes to four. She sat back and waited.

By quarter past four there was still no sign of the

writer and Holly was beginning to think it might be a hoax after all. Not only that, but the reception clerk kept looking across at her. Holly grabbed a magazine from a nearby table and buried her head in it. The last thing she wanted was to draw attention to herself.

Suddenly a shadow was cast across her and a voice said, 'Excuse me, miss.'

At last! thought Holly. She looked up expecting to see the kindly smile from the back cover of P.J. Benson's latest book. Instead she saw the young, curious face of a waitress. 'Is there anything I can get you?' the girl continued.

'No. No, thank you,' Holly said.

The waitress turned towards the reception clerk and shook her head. He shrugged and looked away. Holly felt her cheeks flush red. This must all be a practical joke!

At half past four an elderly woman entered from the street. She seemed to be looking for someone. Holly stared at her. She was older than the photograph and her hair was shorter and bleached blonde. But it could just possibly be the author.

Holly put down the magazine but before she could get to her feet, a girl seated nearby rushed across the room and threw her arms round the old woman.

Holly decided she'd waited long enough. She jumped to her feet and strode angrily towards the entrance. She reached out to open the door, but as she did so a hand gripped her arm. Taken by surprise she turned to find herself looking into the face of a woman in her mid-forties. She had short dark hair and the most amazing emerald green eyes.

'What are you doing here?' the woman said in a low voice as though she was anxious no one else should hear.

Holly tried to shake her arm free of the steely grip. 'You're hurting me,' she said. 'Will you let go please?'

The woman repeated the question. 'What are you doing here?'

'What's it got to do with you?'

'Are you Holly Adams?'

Holly stopped struggling.

'Are you?'

Holly nodded.

'Good,' the woman smiled. 'My name is Benson. P.J. Benson.'

Holly shook her head. 'No, you're not,' she said. 'You're nothing like P.J. Benson. I've seen her picture on the back of her books.'

The woman looked round nervously. 'Don't make a scene, please.'

'Then let go of my arm,' said Holly. 'I don't know what you're up to or who you are, but—'

'No,' the woman interrupted. 'But I know who

you are. You're Holly Adams. Your family moved up here a few months ago from London. You go to the Winifred Bowen-Davies School where you've set up something called the Mystery Club with your two friends Tracy and Belinda. And when you wrote telling me all that and asking for an interview for your school magazine, you called yourself my number one fan.' The woman smiled again. 'Now how would I know that if I wasn't P.J. Benson?'

Holly stared at her. The woman certainly appeared to be telling the truth. Holly nodded. 'All right then.'

'Excuse me.' The reception clerk was standing behind them. He looked puzzled and embarrassed. 'Sorry to bother you, Mrs Payton,' he said. 'But is there anything wrong?'

'Payton?' Holly echoed.

The woman ignored her. 'No, nothing's wrong,' she said. 'This is my niece. We arranged to meet here but there was a mix-up over the time. I just managed to catch her as she was leaving.'

The clerk smiled with relief. 'Oh, good,' he said.

Holly was totally bewildered. She watched the clerk return to the reception desk then she turned back to the woman claiming to be P.J. Benson. 'Mrs Payton!' she said.

'I know it must seem strange,' the woman replied. 'But I really can explain. If you'll only give me a chance. Now please come with me.

I've got a room booked upstairs. We can talk there.'

'No way,' said Holly. 'If you want to explain you can explain down here. And I can tell you now – the explanation had better be good.'